STEPHEN JARED

NEED
MORE
ROAD

Cover Design by Gilles Verschuere

Publisher's Note:

This is a work of fiction. All names, characters, places, and
events are the work of the author's imagination.

Any resemblance to real persons, places, or events is
coincidental.

Solstice Publishing - www.solsticepublishing.com

Need More Road

By Stephen Jared

Chapter One

Eddie Howard spread a square of butter on his toast, watched it melt, and thought about Rock Hudson in *Written on the Wind*. Where did Rock Hudson get his strength and manly stoicism? He thought about Lauren Bacall and Robert Stack. Why would Lauren Bacall marry such a man? She wasn't the type to marry for money. Eddie crunched into his toast as the ticking second hand on the wall clock kept pestering him about the approaching workday. He hated that wall clock. He moved his plate and brushed fallen crumbs onto it with his hand. He planned a repeat viewing this evening. It was Thursday, and on Friday, a new picture would be replacing *Written on the Wind* forever.

After his toast, Eddie peeled a banana. It was the last of a bunch, and dark spots started to form. He took a bite. "Get going," his father's voice told him. He slumped. His parents never went away. He could hear their footsteps, not from ghosts but from memories held as close as the clothes he wore. He could hardly fault them for being ever-present. Not only had he inherited their home, he inherited everything in it. He had been surrounded by their things his whole life. As time passed, the thought of anything new seemed more like the loss of something old.

Breakfast finished, Eddie sat, not moving. It was time to turn off the radio. *Coffee Time at Harmony Homestead* never amused him, but he liked the noise, even though he kept it at a low volume, and it was better than *Rise and Shine* on the television set. He stood, gulped the remainder of his orange juice, stepped to the radio, and clicked it off. The quiet of the old house abruptly consumed everything, even the past. Eddie felt empty, absent the muscles to take him anywhere, absent the heart to care. He sighed, and consoled himself with thoughts of watching Dorothy Malone doing that crazy dance in her bedroom.

After washing his juice glass, and his plate, he returned them to a cupboard. He unplugged the toaster, stared at the electrical socket, and then moved the unplugged toaster a further distance than the length of the cord. Satisfied that no fire could possibly start, Eddie snatched his keys and exited through a back door.

***

The town of Barstow was located in the Mojave Desert, one hundred miles from Los Angeles. Its Main Street was a dusty strip of land hardly unique to small towns, except it had more motels and service stations. For most, it was a fast stop on the way to someplace bigger. Eddie started working at the Security Pacific Bank in 1939, and the building's prominence gave him a nice feeling. He was the assistant manager. His father had been a friend of the manager. Banking suited Eddie. It was repetitive, reliable; not much had changed at the bank since he started.

Although Eddie had a driver's license, he didn't own a car, because he didn't feel he needed one. He preferred to walk. His parents owned a beautiful car, but Eddie saw it as an unnecessary luxury. Sidewalks took him to Main Street, where he landed right next to The Village Hotel & Continental Café. They served Chinese Chop Suey, and Mexican. As every morning, he rounded the corner, tipping his hat to early risers, slowly making his way to the other end of Main Street, where the Security Pacific waited.

It was late October, and plastic pumpkins needed to be topped off with candy before nine o'clock. Skeletons, taped to the windows, danced out in front, and sometimes needed refastening after a night of heavy winds rushed over the desert. Holidays often proved to be a nuisance. Arnold Teesdale, the bank manager, also didn't like holidays. However, he had obligations to the public. It was important, and Eddie agreed, to be trusted and conventional.

Approaching the bank, Eddie recalled a recent confrontation with Mr. Teesdale. It had run through his head many times. Mr. Teesdale's favorite topic was ERMA, a system allowing data sharing between banks. Eddie shrugged it off, didn't care about it, but Mr. Teesdale felt banking would be forever transformed. He talked about it constantly, read everything he could get his hands on regarding its progress. "Once we get ERMA, we won't ever again have problems like this," Mr. Teesdale would say. At times, it was meant to smooth differences; as during the recent confrontation when he said, "I received an unpleasant telephone call from Mr. Hadley's son. His father was refused a withdrawal because his signature didn't match his card."

"Wasn't me," Eddie insisted, immediately annoyed. "Couldn't have been. I've known Hadley for years. Why would I pretend not to?"

"Ray Hadley said it was the frumpy bank man with glasses who refused to recognize the signature, and so refused to extend his father money."

Eddie's irritation increased. "This is ridiculous—"

"Don't make this a drama," Mr. Teesdale snapped at Eddie, his old lips thinning. "I'm just telling you—"

"You know how Hadley gets. He imagines things. He's out of his mind. If his son is so concerned about his father, he should come back here and care for him."

"Look, let's leave it alone. I just wanted you to know—"

"I'm not leaving it alone. If Ray Hadley calls in here, I'm going to tell him what I think."

"You'll do no such thing."

"The man is accusing me of something I never did."

"We both have work to do. You've wasted enough time with this. Besides, once we get ERMA, we won't ever again have problems like this."

Eddie entered at two minutes before nine. From there his day inched forward not unlike most days stretching back over the last seventeen years.

**

Oftentimes, the second viewing of a movie, or even the third, offered more excitement than the first. The characters became familiar, the great ones seemingly real, like friends. Plus, Eddie's anticipation was reinforced with certainty— he already knew the movie was good.

The day had been long and tiring, but Eddie's energies improved once he showered and threw on a short-sleeve button down shirt. He marched to The Barstow, thinking about how much he loved movies. They were everything to him. They expanded his mind, his vision, put a beat in his heart; what would he ever do without them?

"Weren't you here a couple of nights ago?" a uniformed girl asked, as Eddie bought popcorn. Dropping change in his pocket, he pushed through the crowd. Why did she care? Was she being funny? Everyone at The Barstow knew Eddie saw multiple showings a week. He thought of explaining the merits of repeat visits, but the place was packed, and people were standing around. He was also anxious to get his favorite seat.

Eddie liked sitting to the right of center, halfway back from the screen. He sipped Pepsi, shoved popcorn in his face, and waited. After listening in on surrounding conversations, awkward flirting from a young man on a date, news about more heavy winds in the forecast from another, he fell into his own silent conversation. A typically grumpy sort, Eddie became more charitable when seated before a movie screen; even waving friendly to customers he loathed during the day.

Occasionally, he'd see women who, like him, came alone to the movies. He'd wonder about them, fantasize about romance, and then retreat from such imaginings, telling himself their husbands were probably working or playing cards. Eddie rarely looked for rings on fingers. Sometimes he'd see them laugh or cry and he envied the movie-light touching their faces. It wasn't uncommon for him to investigate some of these faces for traces of loneliness when they'd exit The Barstow and head home. This particular night seemed unusual in that he saw no one else so obviously alone as he.

Written on the Wind was again beautiful, the colors more colorful than reality, and though the on-screen lives were filled with torment; Eddie aspired to be like them. They wallowed in luxury, something not only visible in their surroundings, but also in their emotional attachments to each another. The heartbreak to Eddie was leaving them behind. For him nothing was more bittersweet than the crashing finale of a film score and closing credits.

Shuffling through the crowd to a busy sidewalk, Eddie's feet felt heavy but his spirit remained somewhat elevated by the make-believe melodrama. Beneath a fine desert sky, he walked home. Briefly, the comfort of strangers—fellow Thursday night movie fans—sustained his mood. Eventually the crowd thoroughly dispersed, and he walked alone, alongside the high-pitched throb of crickets. His questions about the plot no longer nagged. He couldn't put his finger on why, but things seemed to make more sense. From Main Street, he counted twenty-three lampposts to his house, and when he arrived, he noticed the light fixture above his front door had burned out. Strangely, something about that darkened door added weight to his heart. He felt sad staring at it. After unlocking the backdoor, entering the home, and lighting the rooms, he turned on his television. The grip of solitude began to squeeze, until lessened by *Playhouse 90*. He awoke sometime later to loud hissing and flickering, late-night distortion from his set. He stared as if hypnotized for a moment, the nothingness on the screen staring back, and then he turned it off and went to bed.

***

Fridays were typically good, not bad, but this particular Friday clawed into Eddie's nerves. Polite exchanges all preceded banking questions, endless questions and opinions about accounts, policies, and services. One customer argued the lack of fairness in wealthy people getting better interest rates simply because of large deposits, whereas loyal customers—a customer with ten years at Security Pacific, for instance—paid higher rates. Interest rates were based on risks, Eddie wanted to explain, but he agonized over the thought of offending. In the end, he said, "It's outside my control," and the customer left in a huff. Eddie wanted to say, "So, if a gentleman puts a nickel in a bank for ten years the bank should loan that gentleman twenty thousand dollars because he didn't take his nickel elsewhere?"

Eddie repeatedly grumbled over the exchange—he did this silently—occasionally shaking his head until, at fifteen minutes before lunch, his sister Connie entered. She always came to Eddie with eyes carrying a sizable amount of pity.

"Hi, Eddie." Her face fell to his belly. "Did a button come off? Want me to sew something back on there for you?"

She picked at loose threads on his shirt, and he brushed her hand away, with a fast, "It's okay." Though well intentioned, Connie suffocated him. For years, she repeatedly invited him to her house, even though Eddie mostly turned her down, knowing she would expect reciprocation. She longed for them to be closer. Eddie didn't know why, but he always pulled away.

"What're you up to tonight? Could you use a good meal?" Connie wore a lime-green shirtdress. Her brown hair climbed big and sturdy. The muscles in her chin shoved her lips into a clown smile as she looked up at him.

"Tonight's not the best," Eddie said.

"You have plans?"

The subtle hint of skepticism in her voice rattled him. Agitated further, he reminded her, "You know I don't like going to the movies on Saturday nights. I have to get there too early to get my seat."

"Ann saw you at the movies last night."

"They have a new one opening, and tomorrow night doesn't work for me. Plus, tomorrow night is Halloween."

"What are you doing for Halloween?"

"Nothing."

"Go to the movies then. Most people will be trick-or-treating, spending time with their kids, not at the movies."

"It doesn't work for me."

"Is it that you don't like Lou?"

"What're you talking about? You're my sister. Of course I like Lou. I like the kids. I like everybody. I just want to go to the movies tonight. It's Friday. A new one is opening. I just … it's where I want to be."

Connie turned to Mr. Teesdale, who approached with a friendly greeting calling her Mrs. Ackerman, her married name. Smiling, he said the bank was closing so employees could go to lunch, but Connie convinced him to stay so she could make a deposit. They talked about the upcoming weekend as Mr. Teesdale hustled through the transaction. Connie never had difficulty with small talk. It came naturally to her. Eddie, on the other hand, always had cruel barbs he wrestled into silent submission on his tongue.

Eddie lumbered into the back where an icebox kept his lunch cool. He always ate sitting on a bench across from

Harold B. Seton Elementary. He liked watching the kids throwing balls, crying out. Each day memories returned from when he was a child running around on the same asphalt, making friends, not yet feeling so different.

Today, however, his reflective moods were disrupted by his sister's clinging presence. Her transaction complete, she walked alongside Eddie toward the school. He didn't know how to get rid of her.

"Don't you ever go to lunch with your co-workers?" she asked.

"No."

"Why not?"

"I don't know."

When they sat, Eddie thought it odd she made no mention of the schoolyard. Not only had Connie spent years in the classrooms across the street, but her two kids had as well.

"Eddie, don't you get tired of eating alone?"

"Last week you asked if I get tired of standing all the time." Not one to savor his food, Eddie rapidly chomped through an apple and peanut butter sandwich.

"I just want you to be happy, Eddie."

"I'm fine. The job's fine, been doing it long enough."

With a gentle pat on his forearm, Connie told Eddie that if he changed his mind about dinner they could always make room for him, and then she left. Eddie watched her walk along the hot sidewalk, glad to see her go. From a distance, the industrialized howl of a train cried. Always around lunchtime, going all the way back to his childhood, Eddie could count on the sound of that train. He loved hearing it.

After thirty minutes and a sigh of self-pity, Eddie returned to his customers. Years of working in a bank taught Eddie about money. A man sporting new shoes on a Tuesday didn't smile half as much as the man cashing his check on a Friday. For the most part, the remainder of this Friday offered no surprises, nothing unusual; customers smiled, some complained, and thanks to the hectic pace, hours rolled swiftly. Time seemed to stop, however, when shortly before closing, a woman, clearly from somewhere else, stepped inside. Heads turned to her. The woman fanned her face with a motel brochure. With her other hand she removed dark sunglasses.

Not all at once but relatively quickly, every person in the bank focused their attention her way. Eddie couldn't take his eyes off her. She looked like a movie star. She looked like Marilyn Monroe.

She was not Marilyn of course, nor was this a Halloween act, but she had the same roundness in her chin and cheekbones and hips. She was probably five-ten with high heels and big curls of lemon icing hair. She was a goddess, an undiscovered motion picture goldmine. Eddie thought of approaching, sifting through his brain for a greeting that sounded like Cary Grant, when suddenly Mr. Teesdale rushed to her first.

Eddie neared and listened. He didn't catch the woman's name but did pick up that she was seeking a home to buy for her father. She was from Los Angeles. She didn't mention an occupation, didn't mention a husband. She said she thought she'd stop in at the bank and see if the bank folks were friendly. She smiled a lot. She seemed unaware of the irritated, disapproving looks from other women in the bank. She soon left, not with a walk, but with a swaying, swinging movement, no bones, pure softness.

She was gone. Thoughts slowed once she left. Eddie's face hung. He couldn't concentrate. Impaired now, Eddie referred to a local townswoman as Trudy when he'd known for years her name was Gladys. He worried for a moment Mr. Teesdale might have overheard the mistake, but the old man was snickering with a customer, no doubt about the woman who had captured everyone's notice.

Even after closing, Eddie couldn't stop thinking about her. *A Kiss Before Dying* opened at The Barstow that night. Eddie was there, popcorn in hand, his favorite place, yet he was heavy-hearted, trapped in a cloud of loneliness thanks to a beautiful woman's three minutes inside the Security Pacific.

***

The next morning, Eddie worked. He worked a short day every Saturday. It was a weekly routine he started in 1951. It marked one of the few changes Eddie could recall since all the way back to 1939.

Sue, a pear-shaped teller who, like Eddie, had been at the Security Pacific for years, once spent nine days away from the bank. She was shocked and distraught after a customer grabbed his chest, fell to the carpet, and died. Sue's husband said she couldn't stop crying. Everyone hugged her when she returned, even Eddie.

Lynette looked like a bird, always snacking, obsessively crunching, throwing her head back, and dropping more of this or that down her throat. It drove Eddie crazy. The three of them worked Saturday mornings in the back room on huge adding machines and manually updated paper ledgers for account holders. Each employee posted roughly two hundred accounts per hour.

Eddie was faster than the others. It didn't bother him though, as the added time allowed his mind to drift. Silently, Eddie again considered that *Written on the Wind* was very colorful. It used color artfully. Many recent color pictures seemed to be in color solely for profit. Some months back, Eddie had a conversation with Buddy Siefert, the manager of The Barstow, and he said there wouldn't be anymore black and white pictures after a few more years, and Eddie believed that would be a terrible loss. While many color pictures were beautiful, the black and white pictures offered further distance from reality and Eddie liked that very much.

When finished with work on this Saturday, Eddie tossed a dull, "Happy Halloween," to Sue and Lynette as the two women headed off to Chester's Cafeteria for lunch. With a brown sack-lunch in one hand and a set of keys in the other, Eddie locked the bank. He then rattled the handle three times to be certain the mechanisms fastened before starting down the sidewalk. After a few steps, he turned, went back, and gave the door a fourth tug.

Across the street the stunning platinum blond from the day before walked. Stepping off the sidewalk where there was no intersection, she headed for the bank. She moved with poise, and Eddie, squinting in the sun, thought that walking must be among her favorite things. Her dress was the color of cream-filled coffee with white polka dots. He panicked as he thought of speaking to her. He grabbed his glasses, and rubbed them clean with his tie.

"Hi."

She had a funny way of speaking, sounded surprised by everything. Eddie only really got a full earful of it when she said, "I was hoping to speak with the manager. Did I come at a bad time? You're not closing, are you?"

Returning his glasses to his head, Eddie cleared his throat, took a breath, and muttered, "It's ... um ... Saturday. We close at noon. Actually, we're not open. We don't open on Saturdays. But some of us work, you know ..." Eddie shook his head, frustrated with his nerves.

"It's Saturday?" she marveled. "I guess I'm all turned around."

"We'll be open Monday morning."

"Monday? Oh, of course." Her shoulders slumped, and face fell into a child's pout. "Oh, I wish I hadn't gotten confused." She put a long fingernail between her teeth. Her eyes fell within.

"You ... um ... you have a question? I might be able to answer it. I've worked here a while."

"Why bring a sack-lunch?"

"Beg pardon?"

"Well, I mean, it's none of my business, but why not just go home and eat?"

"I like to eat down the street," Eddie replied awkwardly. "There's a bench."

"That sounds like a peaceful way to spend a break in the day." She swiveled on her hips as she spoke. A light wind touched her sculpted blonde curls. The hand near her face rested at the top of her dress, and the curve of her forearm matched the sinuous lines that seemed to come at him from everywhere. "My name is Mary Rose."

"I'm Edward, Eddie, Howard," he said, and then added, "You could be in movies, you know? I'm sure people tell you that."

"A couple of years ago I saw Linda Darnell at the Crescendo on Sunset Boulevard. I didn't know the man she was with until someone told me his name was Mankiewicz, and I guess he's somebody, and I guess they had been having an affair. They were married at the time to other people, or at least he was, I'm not sure. Anyway, I had this sudden flash where for a brief moment I thought, this must be what it feels like to be a star."

"Boy, that's something."

"Listen, Eddie—may I call you Eddie?—I don't want to hold you up. May I walk with you to that bench of yours, and I can ask a couple of questions? You don't mind, do you?" When she smiled her eyes smiled before her lips. A brightening expression pinched them and they sparkled. Eddie felt special to be at the heart of her interest if only for a short time. "My daddy plans to open an account, and we were wondering if he needed to be present, or can I open the account for him, and then have him Western Union the money over?"

"Oh … well, I suppose … um … Western Union is for transferring and … um … of course telegrams and stuff." Despite the odd question, Eddie answered with a polite and professional voice. "The account would already have to exist. You could open an account in your name and your father could transfer money into your account, but if you wanted the account in your father's name he would have to come in on his own and set that up."

"I see. You really know your stuff. I'm impressed. Say, your manager was awfully friendly with me."

"Mr. Teesdale?"

"Yes. He said this is a wonderful place."

"He never works on Saturdays."

"Why not?"

"I guess he thinks he's the best with the customers," Eddie replied as they walked. "Probably is. I don't know."

"Do you like living here?"

"I've never lived anywhere else. I think he trusts me with the numbers too. Mr. Teesdale. I've never made mistakes, no horrible ones anyway."

"Seems a nice place to settle."

"Are you moving here?"

"Once my daddy gets situated, I'll decide if I want to stay."

Eddie caught the scent of perfume. He weakened with her nearness. What must it be like to touch her, he wondered, and then sank into shame as a vision of a kiss teased his reality.

They sat on the hot bench. She talked and smiled a lot. The schoolyard was empty of play, just lifeless metal swings and slides. The sun cooked Eddie, irritating him more than usual. He set his sack-lunch aside, not eating it. He just listened, and kept wondering how she had come to him. Would she mock him later? What thoughts passed through that come-hither head of hers?

"He's retired now, my daddy. He worked on the railroads. Oh, we moved around a lot, let me tell you. I've lived everywhere. His daddy, my granddaddy, lived in Los

Angeles. That's where we lived the last few years. Oh, it's real nice there. Anyway, he just died, my granddaddy. It was very sad. But he had a lot of money. That's the reason I came into the bank yesterday. I had to make sure everything looks to be handled by serious people. Say, I don't have any friends around here. Would you be my friend? Maybe you'd like to show me around? Is it just the one street? Why aren't you eating your lunch? Please don't think it rude. You must be hungry. Most of my life has been devoted to my daddy. I love him very much, and with moving around and all, I haven't met anyone … Say, I have an idea! Oh, it would be such fun! Would you go trick-or-treating with me tonight? We won't ask for candy like the little ones. We'll just dress up. It'll be fun. How about it?"

***

Eddie stood alone, feeling nervous, even incredulous while waiting to be met by someone who looked like she could be in pictures. He was in the lobby of the Town & Country Motel holding a plastic sword. The Town & Country was a lengthy walk from stores and restaurants, yet still on Main Street. It provided more expansive land and sky, always thought to be one of the fancier places to stay. Through windows, Eddie could see the horizon cutting a dramatic line across the desert. Above low distant mountains, the remaining daylight burned beneath stars. The view felt sad and beautiful at the same time.

Eddie reminded himself to let go of the little things that bothered him. Relax, adopt a stoic demeanor, he told himself, but he felt overwhelmed by the task. Shifting from the western view, he sighed, turned, and caught the lustrous blue of the pool. A moment later, walking alongside the pool, heading toward him, was Mary Rose.

Hugging her were high waist, slim pants. A cool azure reached from the pool and touched her, shimmering happily all over her body. The pants were white and extended to just below her knees. Her top was skintight, short-sleeve. She held a folded sheet.

The motel clerk near the pool straightened as she passed. Eddie heard her thank the man, calling him "darling," and then she flaunted the folded sheet in his smiling face before stepping into the lobby. "Where's your costume?" she asked with that surprised voice of hers.

Eddie held up his sword. "I also have an eye-patch."

Her eyes pressed and sparkled, smiling a split second before giddiness extended to her mouth. She went to him, slid an arm under his, and guided him. "They were nice enough to give me an old sheet, which I managed to poke two cute little holes into so I can see."

"A ghost?"

"Of course, silly."

As they reached the street, a Buick Super with its top down passed and blasted its horn. Baffled, aggravated, Eddie said, "Boy, what got into them, you wonder?"

A coy Mary Rose met his question. He felt suddenly ridiculous. He didn't say anything for a while. They walked. The heat of the day held stubbornly. Eddie decided to let the wicked indulgence of the evening excuse the men in the car. He tried to put it out of his mind, but then asked, "I guess that must happen a lot?"

"I don't look for that kind of attention. I wish it didn't happen. I guess it should be something I feel flattered by but instead it makes me feel frightened, and like someone who goes out of their way to get attention, and I'm not like that. There doesn't seem to be much I can do about it."

"It's not nice."

"Say, I've got an idea." She unfolded her sheet, and a moment later was a ghost. Stretching out her arms, she made comical ghostly howls. "Put on your eye-patch," she demanded.

Her exquisite beauty was now Eddie's secret, and he felt happier. They soon strolled along the sidewalks of the town and around homes. Someone recognized Eddie from the bank and inquired about his mystery companion. To which Eddie joked that he didn't see anyone.

The hidden Mary Rose came out. She enjoyed spooking little ones. She had a cackling laugh, endearingly grating to the ears. She's a girl again, thought Eddie, and he quickly became less intimidated.

"What's your favorite movie," he asked.

"Oh, I don't often see movies."

"Well, I only know two subjects, movies and banking, and since I refuse to discuss the nuances of financial investment that leaves the conversation to you."

"Okay, let me think." For a long time she paused, walking unseen except for her eyes. "When I was a little girl," she finally said, "people mistook me for a boy."

"I can't imagine."

"Oh, it's true, let me tell you. I made a friend—this is when we lived in Clarksburg—and he was a little boy. He thought I was a boy too. I had short hair, and for some reason my parents dressed me in short pants. This was just before the war, and someone who had a boy who grew too big for them probably gave the pants to them. I let him believe I was a boy because I had no friends. Thomas was his name. We went to the circus. We played marbles. One day I said something and he looked at me funny. He was quiet all afternoon. I tried to get him to talk but couldn't. We'd been playing together for weeks by that point. Anyway, he finally said to me—I'll never forget it—he said, 'You're a girl, aren't you?' and I was heartbroken. I thought he would no longer be my friend."

"What happened?"

"Well, he did come to my house again but I stayed in my room. I never played with him again."

"I'm sorry."

"Oh, it's nothing. We moved a short time later but when I see little girls and boys running around playing I often think back to that."

The mood of everyone seemed to crackle with gaiety for a couple of hours. Halloween had become a bigger thing since he was a boy, Eddie thought, relishing every moment with this surprising woman and the sight of so many devils and ghouls running around them.

At around eight, the quiet of a normal Saturday evening had mostly returned. At Main Street, they headed back toward the edge of town. They mentioned the warm winds, "Not like chilly Los Angeles nights," she said, and the "fingernail shape of the moon," as Eddie tapped his plastic sword to the brick storefronts they passed.

When they arrived back at the Town & Country, Mary Rose pulled the sheet off, saying, "Want to come to my room for a whiskey?" Some of her blonde fell out of perfection. She shook her locks, giggled, and Eddie thought he'd not seen her so enticing. What did she really want? What did she see in Eddie? Ladies didn't invite strange men into their motel rooms.

"Halloween seems to get bigger every year," she said, opening the door to room seven.

"I was thinking the same thing," Eddie responded. He watched her find a lamp in the darkness. The room smelled fresh. Everything looked new and clean.

"Certainly since I was little," she went on. "Of course, they wouldn't let us trick-or-treat during the war." She closed the door and locked it.

"Oh, right," Eddie remembered. She removed her shoes. He watched her dart to a cabinet in bare feet, and when she stood there with her back to him, he allowed his eyes the full luxury of her. He couldn't think clearly, warned himself against his own thoughts, and determined every word hanging on his lips to be agonizingly inadequate.

"Do you like ice?"

Unsure how to respond—he never drank whiskey—he said, "However you, whatever you want."

"I'd have to go get ice. I prefer mine without. When I have ice in it I drink it too fast."

"I don't need ice."

"Sit down," she said, gesturing to a small table with chairs. "I had so much fun tonight. Thanks for putting up with me, Eddie."

She brought two glasses, and they sat with the table between them. She crossed her legs, and said, "Tell me about yourself, Eddie. You seem interesting."

Eddie shifted, saw her sip her whiskey, and then moved his eyes off. "Oh, I'm …I'm … I had a good time tonight, too."

"Good."

"I'm not that interesting."

There was a narrowing of her eyes. What did they see? He took a swift drink, coughed from the burning, and when he tried to speak, it was difficult. "I was surprised when you said you don't have many friends."

"My daddy's protective."

Breath on fire, Eddie then pressed, "But he let you come here."

"For a couple of days." In a flirtatious manner she added, "How much trouble could I get in?"

His stomach tightened. He scrutinized her words. What did she want? Eddie had a hard time responding. He'd never encountered anything like this before. What should he do? What should he say? At last he posed a question without phrasing it as a question. "You're here with me."

She uncrossed her legs, leaned forward, close enough for him to smell her perfume, and then she briefly dropped her eyes before lifting them again to Eddie. "I can tell you aren't going to try anything. You don't look at me the way other men do. Your eyes show respect."

Eddie felt surprisingly liberated, and pleased that his behavior seemed so agreeable. Anxieties quieted. They talked about scary movies. He couldn't get over how few pictures she'd seen. He was roughly twice her age, but as some of the favorites from his youth were now playing on television, he figured maybe she'd seen a few. She laughed at things he said, and he was glad he'd decided not to run from this experience.

The evening ended with them in her automobile listening to *The Shadow* on the radio. Without a radio in her room, Mary Rose grabbed her keys when Eddie mentioned with some excitement that they were missing it. With windows down they listened, smiling, looking out at a high moon shining above, and the cool glow of the pool waiting for the sun.

***

The couch-pillow Eddie's head sunk into as he awoke had an aged but not unpleasant smell, as if stuffed with cozy memories. *Gospel Caravan* was on the television, its music representing a world Eddie knew little about. He stretched, rubbed his eyes with his palms, and massaged his head. Sitting up, he looked curiously at the singers in their sharp clothes.

He showered, dressed, and had his toast and banana while the radio played. Accompanied by the clanging of church bells, he began his Sunday routine. He mowed the grass, trimmed hedges, dusted and vacuumed the house. When finished with all that, he ate lunch. After that, he rested, tried to nap, but couldn't. Something was different.

He kept replaying Saturday night in his head, and wondered what she was doing, what she was thinking. Would he see her again? He imagined her on the telephone with someone in Los Angeles, complaining about boredom and uninteresting people. A woman like Mary Rose had to have friends, he thought. Men hounded her; they had to—tough men, good-looking men, movie stars, and everyone else. Who was she on the telephone with? Another man would have pulled her into his arms and kissed her. She would have welcomed it. She would have melted. Another man would still be with her on Sunday. Another man would've told her what to do, and she would've been willing. She would've been happy to please. These unwelcome thoughts raced through Eddie's mind while he remained unmoving.

The chatty voice then reminded him it wasn't another man who was with her the previous night. He, Eddie Howard, was with her. After a while, he changed clothes and hustled off. He wanted to see if she was still at the Town & Country. If she spotted him, he'd be embarrassed; nevertheless, unable to think about anything else, he went. He couldn't stop himself. Crazy as it seemed, he needed to know she remained near. Marching along sidewalks under a dim twilight sky, he noticed Halloween was over. Yesterday's decorations were gone. How had the night passed so quickly? he wondered.

Maybe his stopping by wouldn't be strange. Maybe she was lonely, thinking about him. Maybe she too had funny engines inside she just couldn't shut down. Counting steps as he walked, he convinced himself that someone as beautiful as she couldn't possibly find him appealing. He was making a terrible mistake, and the embarrassment would spread all over town.

At Main Street, he halted. To his left was the movie house playing *A Kiss Before Dying*. To his right, further down the road, was the Town & Country. Maybe she met some handsome traveler, a man of her dreams. Maybe a wealthy doctor was also new to the area, and they struck up a conversation by the pool. What to do? Hadn't he seen enough movies? he asked himself. He'd seen *A Kiss Before Dying* within the last week. He'd seen hundreds of movies over the years. To pursue Mary Rose at least promised something new, something real, if even a broken heart, and to put his eyes on her for even a minute more seemed worth the price of her thinking him a fool. So he continued.

Headlights from passing automobiles swept his elongated shadow across the desert floor. Each shadow rushed backwards as if telling him to retreat, run home. It was a smart shadow, much like the radio program, he thought. Nevertheless, he pressed on, bracing himself for humiliation.

Before long, he arrived at the Town & Country, ambling into the parking lot. Motels always had vacancies on Sunday nights, so it was no surprise to see few cars. Mary Rose's 1952 Pontiac Chieftain was gone. The parking spot she had was empty. It was devastating. Where did she go? Los Angeles? Would he never see her again? The likeliness was agonizing. Compelled to check her room, Eddie glanced into the lobby, didn't see anyone, and so he rounded the pool and entered a hallway. The door to room seven was open. His heavy face lifted. However, just as he was about to enter, the motel clerk exited the room pushing a vacuum. Quickly pivoting, Eddie dashed off.

Stomping toward the street, cursing his rotten life, he felt pain more intense than he'd even predicted. It was more than the woman who'd left him; it was the realization that he'd never experienced such feelings before. His whole life had been lost, wasted, empty, and he only now saw it clearly.

A flash alarmed him. Headlights, steady now, charged at him. He dodged, stumbling out of the way. Brakes squealed. The Chieftain stopped. It was Mary Rose.

"Eddie?"

"Wha—What're you—"

"You almost ran into me."

Confused, Eddie only stared.

Swinging her door out, she burst upward with some astonishment, and continued, "I was on my way back to Los Angeles."

"Oh …"

"The wind was blowing my hair every which way, and I realized I didn't have my scarf. I came back, thinking I must've left it in the room."

"The man was just cleaning it," Eddie said.

"My room?"

"Yeah, I saw him."

Mary Rose snapped across the pavement in heels. She wore a sleeveless shirt and narrow pants that went to her ankles. Eddie followed. She talked fast, speaking of the sentimental value of the scarf, irreplaceable, belonged to her mother, and she had to find it. They met the clerk, who also seemed pleased by her return, and he unlocked the door to her room, said he hadn't seen her scarf, but she was welcome to search, he would be in the lobby if needed.

The room looked nice, neat, smelled icy, much like before. Eddie felt his life had become like a movie. He was Dean Martin chasing a ditzy bombshell. He couldn't remember being so excited. It was now too late to drive to Los Angeles, she said. She would stay, would have to call her daddy. She looked in a closet, but it was empty. She spun around, moved curtains, tried behind a dresser, voiced her frustration, and then got down on her knees to look under the bed. Eddie watched her wazoo lift high in the air. She lingered. Her backside swayed as she shifted. She talked more, mentioned rummaging through the Chieftain out in the desert somewhere, also said she didn't have much from her mother's belongings.

Gingerly, while standing over her, Eddie bent his knees and ever so delicately—he couldn't help himself— put a hand to her lower back. The gesture was impulsive. He thought he might excuse it as a consoling touch.

Mary Rose pulled a perplexed glare from under the bed and faced Eddie very directly with it. He had taken his hand back, stopped breathing, appalled by what he'd done. A boundary had been crossed. Eddie felt certain she was about to tell him how beastly he'd been. Instead, she said nothing.

She got back to her feet, let out a sigh, and expressed further bewilderment regarding the scarf. Eddie had a hard time speaking after what he'd done. Despite the fact that he'd only touched her back, he still felt ashamed. He wanted to go. He hated himself. Within minutes, he complained of being tired and lumbered home.

***

On Monday morning, Eddie felt better. He kept to his routine but his mind was filled with new thoughts. He saw himself breezing through a door into a fast kiss, reading newspapers while seated in the cabin of a speeding train, buying airline tickets to Cairo. She was always at his side. She never left him, and never would. He baffled customers at the Security Pacific, as when Mrs. Trevor entered with her two youngest and asked, "How was your Halloween, Mr. Howard?" and he answered, "Fantastic. Unbelievable."

At lunch, unable to hold back, he hurried to the Town & Country. He had to see her no matter the risk of appearing ridiculous. Any sensible person would've advised against it, he knew. She had become an addiction but worse than gambling or alcohol, she might never be available again. He hoped she had not yet left, even made a rare request to God for it to be so. Arriving at her door, sweating, rehearsing an invite to The Barstow, he paused before knocking so he could catch his breath. Finally, he tapped with his knuckles a few times and waited. For a moment, he worried she might not be alone, and then the door opened.

"Oh, Eddie." Her body was wrapped in a white towel, with another atop her head like a turban. "I was just talking on the telephone. Come in."

Eddie remained unmoving. "I'm on break," he mumbled. "I got to get back. I thought maybe you'd, if you're still around, I had an idea. I don't know if you're, if you'll say yes, but I was thinking, you know, we have a movie theater in town."

"You want to take me to the movies?"

"When are you going back to Los Angeles?"

"My daddy said—he was who I was on the telephone with—he's coming in the next few days, and he said that I should just wait for him. No sense in making the long drive."

The rushing fantasies were such that Eddie kept his eyes off her until finally, unable to prevent it, he braved another look. She tilted her face sideways, held her radiant smile, and began to swivel her hips enticingly. "So, we can spend as much time together as you like."

That afternoon, back at the bank, Eddie was talkative, much more so than usual. Customers didn't irritate him. He even felt sympathy for some, like one poor fellow whose wife huffed and swore, stood in line with arms crossed like Mussolini every time she did her banking. Mr. Teesdale's wife too, though pleasantly mannered compared to her husband, looked like a can-opener. Her teeth splayed as if desperately fleeing bad breath. Meanwhile, excruciatingly aware he was no Cary Grant, Eddie was spending evenings with the most beautiful woman he'd ever seen. How was it possible?

He had always been different, not like most people, and she was different too. Maybe that was the simple secret as to why they'd found each other. Maybe she saw something in him she had never seen in another man.

She wore a halter neck print dress that night. Her soft bare shoulders were unblemished. Eddie's eyes discreetly rolled over her every sensuous impossible curve, and every stolen glance melted Eddie into a puddle, yet his prurience thundered.

At The Barstow, she put a delicate hand beneath Eddie's arm. Was she seeking his protection? Eddie didn't know what to make of it. He was agitated by the intense scrutiny from others. Eyes combed her from top to bottom. The other patrons, the townspeople, amazingly had no regard for maintaining public decorum. They were disrespectful. Eddie waited on popcorn until lights went down, preferring instead to find seats and escape the staring.

For the second time in only four days, Eddie watched *A Kiss Before Dying*. In his world, there was nothing unusual about revisiting a picture so quickly, however, for the first time he had no interest in the make-believe played out before him. His thoughts were solely on Mary Rose.

Later, he told her about Connie and how he didn't like her husband, Lou, "but they have kids," he said, as if the little ones were a lock on a cage. He talked about his dad, mentioning how during the war Eddie felt guilty about staying at the bank. "You're the last person they need over there," his dad said, referring to the overseas conflicts. Such few words, and yet they became a prick to Eddie's heart he still felt. He hoped these minor confessions would crack a window from which she could express vulnerabilities but all of her secrets remained locked within.

Escorting her back to the Town & Country, Eddie acted the gentleman. He imagined himself like Rock Hudson. When he got home, he thought briefly of turning on the television but instead went to bed. He lay there most of the night, not sleeping, wondering about her, feeling life starting at last.

Chapter Two

Eddie sat in the passenger seat while Mary Rose drove. They hummed along Highway 58 seeking Route 395. Death Valley burned like a furnace to the north. An end-of-the-day sun lingered, its final moments seeming to have powers of purification. The skin on their faces, the road, rugged miles of dry land, and everything else turned the same color as a barrel of oranges. With her sweet hands on the wheel, Mary Rose's beauty was flushed with excitement. The windows were down, and wind blew perfume all around inside the Chieftain.

Eddie tried remembering the name of the girl in the fifth grade who smelled so good. He had sat behind her, hands gripped to the edges of his desk, intoxicated by the long hair that drifted in silky waves down her back. She was really something. How many kids were in that class? What happened to her?

"Ever been on an airplane?" Mary Rose asked, breaking a comfortable silence. They had talked a lot in the handful of days following their night at The Barstow. She remained elusive, coy. How smart was she? Not very, he had decided. She was awfully young though, and that could account for some things. Eddie opened up about his insecurities and fears, and how he viewed most people's actions as masked performances played to the expectations of those around them. "Stepping off that stage doesn't take you anywhere though," he had added. "It puts you in darkness."

He saw the two of them as misfits. He suspected turmoil within her, something unsettled, a dark secret perhaps. It seemed to reach out to him, and though she may have only instinctively understood this connection between them, it was the reason they spent so much time together. Now he was her passenger, silently pleading to be taken anywhere, preferably someplace far, free from sameness, free from predictability and stability, and all the things he'd forever known.

As he contemplated her question, movie images flashed through his mind. He thought how he'd love to tell adventurous stories of air travel. "No. Have you?"

"No, but I want to."

"Me too."

"I sometimes imagine soaring through clouds on the way to someplace far," Mary Rose said, and Eddie wondered if she'd read his thoughts. "How wonderful it would be to disappear, go to some foreign place where they don't even speak English, and no one knows you, and start life again."

"That sure would be something," was all Eddie could think to say.

For a while, they returned to their own thoughts, Eddie's mind shuffling through the years for some daring experience to communicate, and then Mary Rose swung her chin his way, asking, "Have you ever done anything really bad?"

He wondered what she expected of him. Was she seeking to confess past deeds? What, in her mind, constituted something really bad? "You mean like cheat on a test or something?"

"Oh, I don't know. I suppose I'm getting carried away. I've rarely felt so free. I love my daddy, of course, but being with him all the time has been limiting. I've always done exactly what was expected of me. Sometimes I think I'd like to do something really wild."

"Like what?"

"I don't know."

***

Sunlight faded. Eddie felt stars swarming in his head, lifting him to a higher elevation. Mary Rose and he stood amid nothing but desert. She had taken them off 395, dodged ditches and shrubs, parked safely, and now the white of the moon lit their small tender footsteps along hardened unfamiliar ground. Something special was happening. Eddie felt dizzy from the possibilities before him, and the lost lonely life watching him from behind. Mary Rose looked at him with a giggle she wouldn't release. What was she thinking? Warm night air offered a breath and her dress quivered. What were they doing out in the middle of nowhere?

"Do you like me, Eddie?"

Too bewildered for words, he nodded. He then watched her climb onto the back of the Chieftain and embrace a star-filled night seemingly lit for them alone.

"Better than movies, don't you think, Eddie?"

"I suppose so," he managed.

"Come up here with me and look straight into the sky."

Carefully, Eddie climbed up and stretched out like her, hands clasped behind his head, facing a million worlds beyond. He felt like a pupil, learning how easy it could be to take a different road now and then, see something different, or see the same things in a new way. Their skin and clothes became assorted shades of blue. She was right about the stars; pictures couldn't capture such majesty.

"Feels like you're in space, doesn't it?"

"Mm-hmm … or on a ship maybe. A ship out at sea." Indeed, Eddie felt a sense of floating. Gentle waves carried him, drifting him into a deep blue, far away and peaceful, dreaming, a place from which he never wished to return.

"Once when I was a little girl—it must've been one of the first times I was left alone—in the middle of the day, I got so scared. My mother was still around. She and daddy went off somewhere. I worried no one was coming back for me. Have I been abandoned? I felt my heart racing. I began to panic. I started to cry. I don't remember what gave me the idea, but I went outside, through the backdoor, into the middle of the yard, and I lay down in the grass, flat on my back, and stared up at the sky. It was a beautiful summer day. The sky was a pretty blue with white clouds slowly floating by. It calmed me. I don't know why but even though I was alone, the vastness of the sky made me feel less lonely."

Eddie didn't say anything. Thoughts raced. He shared her fear of solitude, and yet he forever longed to be alone. Why? What contradictory spirits possessed him? Why such distance with Connie?

A butterfly crossed their star-filled vision, skipping in short bursts on the night air. Eddie pointed at it then dropped his hand. They both watched, following easily as the bright moon lit its wings.

"You don't usually see them at night," Eddie said, careful with his volume.

"He's so beautiful."

"How do you know it's a he?"

"Aren't males supposed to be more beautiful?"

"I don't know. I don't know anything about butterflies."

"I don't know either. I don't know much of anything. But I do remember that a butterfly's lifespan is only a month. Isn't that sad? Shame that something so lovely can be around only for a short time."

Eddie fell silent, hearing the mature resignation in her voice. He worried that he might've been wrong about her intellect, maybe she was smarter than he, more willing to let things go, that her feelings about life and the world were more normal than he previously thought. He focused on the sky, seeking serenity in the stars. At that moment, her hand rested on his, squeezing softly, then simply holding his hand over warm metal.

***

Morning began its slow rise, taking stars down from what might have been the best night of Eddie's life. He felt merely a little tired, not much, prompting further astonishment, as he saw the sharpening angles of rooftops and trees through the windows of The Continental. He sipped orange juice, wolfishly chomped on sunny-side-up eggs, bacon, pancakes, and cinnamon toast while Mary Rose more delicately worked her way through sliced peaches, scrambled eggs, biscuits with marmalade, and a coffee with sugar and cream. Feeling orphaned from his routines unsettled Eddie, but he kept telling himself something important was happening. Her presence tossed a key into his prison. She made him feel like a kid again. He hated acknowledging how devoted to her he'd become. He hated the idea of being without her. How had this happened so quickly?

"Another thing I missed last night was *The Bob Cummings Show*. Where do you suppose they film that?"

"Los Angeles."

"Right there, huh?" Eddie's face crinkled up in wonder. "Wow. That's amazing."

"My daddy is driving to Barstow soon."

Unsure of the expected response, Eddie simply said, "That'll be nice for you."

"Yes."

"I can't believe you've never watched *Dragnet*. I'm sure we missed a real quality program last night with that one. It's so realistic you just can't believe it."

"Is that right?"

"Well, they show you what it's really like."

"I'm sure you can catch those shows next Friday night if you want to."

Though Eddie detected nothing cross in her tone, he felt Mary Rose's words were similar to things his father would sometimes say to his mother when his patience had hit a wall. From Mary Rose he waited apprehensively for a clear sign she was upset, but none came. "I had a wonderful time last night," he added finally.

Eddie thought back to when his mom used to get upset watching their dog dribble water all over the kitchen floor. She'd follow the dog throughout the house, saying, "I just bet he's going into the kitchen to get a drink and I'll have to clean it up." One night Dad was angry, and after Mom wiped the floor for what must have been the hundredth time that day, he went to the water bowl and flipped it over. Mom cried out but was quickly overpowered by Dad's volume as he screamed, "Now you won't look like a crazy person wiping the floor all night! Go ahead! There's a spill for you! Have a great time!" Mom ran off as she often did, marching through the neighborhood, quickly rubbing tears from her cheeks so no one would guess her home wasn't a happy one.

"I had a nice time too," Mary Rose said.

"I don't have to watch those shows next week."

"You should do what you want to, Eddie."

Eddie sighed. What was she thinking? After a lengthy pause, he asked, "What are you going to do today?"

"As soon as I get back to my room I'm going to take a nap. What time do you have to be at the bank?"

"A couple of hours from now."

"I'm sorry to have kept you out all night. I didn't mean to."

Her sweet consideration touched him. He wished he could get out of work. Should he call in sick? She needed sleep, Eddie told himself. He'd likely just pace around anyway, wondering about her, waiting for her to wake up. Hours later, Eddie sat at his desk with a customer, the previous evening sitting on his shoulder like a dream.

"Are there projections as to population growth? My wife and I can relocate to a city, but we'd prefer to stay, and I've been reading about the number of new homes …"

On occasion Eddie sat listening to a young person planning a future—this happened a lot at the bank—and in these moments, feelings of inferiority hammered him like a torrential rain. Why didn't he have plans when he was young? Why didn't he have a wife? Why would an assistant manager at the only bank in town stay home during the most celebrated social events of the year?

"Twenty-seven percent," Mr. Teesdale interrupted. Eddie's boss had come out of nowhere. "Housing is up twenty-seven percent with most new construction in suburban areas."

"I just want to be sure I'll have enough business," the young man said in response to Mr. Teesdale.

"The economy is growing at a rate of seven point six percent. Say, why don't you come over to my desk? I was just going through these numbers with another customer."

The scrawny youth with neatly combed Brylcreem hair followed Mr. Teesdale's guiding hand away from Eddie. Before stepping away, Mr. Teesdale leaned to Eddie and whispered, "How many times have I said read the newspapers? You need to know what's going on. You have to encourage people to take a loan. Staring at them and saying nothing won't get you anywhere. I'm telling you, if something happens to me, they'll have to bring in a manager from someplace else, because you, if you were manager, would drive this bank right out of business."

When these attacks came, and they came frequently, Eddie felt powerless to defend himself. The difficulty was that deep down he truly didn't care about the business. For a while, over a decade earlier, Mr. Teesdale nudged delicately, offering tender encouragement. He thought he could mold Eddie into a younger version of himself. Having failed, he grew to dislike Eddie intensely. He treated him with contempt. What could be done about it?

Eddie asked himself. If respect was not earned from decency and loyalty, did he even want it?

At mid-day, Eddie sat at his lunch bench listening to the distant giddy screams of children across the street. They hopped on concrete and fearlessly climbed metal bars. Many ran as if chased by no one or nothing Eddie could see. From one side of the playground to the other, they ran every which way, as fast as their legs would take them.

A November breeze relaxed the intense sunshine, adding to a growing fatigue. An airplane flew over, reminding him of the previous day's conversation with Mary Rose. What would it feel like to be up there on that plane? To be part of the expanding world, meeting different people, seeing things, must be a thrill, he thought. It never matched his temperament though, to add actions to curiosity. He realized that Mary Rose's sudden presence challenged his pragmatism, or whatever it was preventing him from taking a single step in a new direction.

Eddie sighed and bit into his peanut butter sandwich. How had so many years passed as if he wasn't part of them? He wished he could get them back. Confounding his spiraling disconsolation was the sense of a presence lurking over his shoulder, telling him he didn't have the strength to change, the fortitude needed to become someone new, or even take a step in a new direction, wasn't built into him. Plus, in a few years he'd be fifty. As he looked back throughout most of his melancholic life, he realized he was anchored in things he believed would never change. Why? When had this paralysis started? He'd suffered no single traumatic event as a child. He simply started turning away from everything at some point. Why? He had missed so much. What caused him to dodge what others naturally gravitated toward? He had nothing. He had only his mother and father's house, the same rooms he'd been lumbering through his whole life.

He felt a flush of emotion and thought tears might come, and so he stood. Determined for once in his life to make a grand move impulsively, he dropped an uneaten apple in a nearby trashcan, and then marched off to Armstrong's Jewelers. He hadn't stepped inside the place since picking up his high school class ring in 1928. He smiled at the thought of Mary Rose's surprised face. Was he out of his mind? He fantasized that she would marry him. If not, he will have made the effort, he told himself. He will have tried.

"Mr. Howard, what're you doing here?" a voice shouted from a back room where the sun didn't catch. The front door had a sharp tinny bell, unnerving Eddie. It clamored again as he shut the door. Appearing in a spotlight angling through a high window, behind display cases, looking slightly familiar, wearing a floral dress, and holding a piece of knitting, a woman greeted him again without any diminishing of friendliness. "Planning on getting hitched, Mr. Howard?" she asked, before releasing an extended chuckle.

Her husband did the banking. His name was Abe, and he came in routinely, Eddie recalled. What was her name? Eddie knew her from way back. Did he go to school with her? Why was she laughing? Was he a joke? What did people say about him behind his back?

"Hello ..." He put some courage behind his step. "I was just ..." Wedding rings were hundreds of dollars, he reminded himself. He'd have to pay a little at a time. He was still a stranger to Mary Rose's father. "You know what? Never mind. I'm sorry. I don't know what I was ..." Eddie pivoted and left, striking that bell again with the door.

Hands in his pockets, head fallen forward, he walked back to work. With every step, he kicked through a sun-blasted haze of reluctance. He hated his life. He wished for everything to be different, yet how could he become someone entirely new? Nothing around him was new. The whole town had been the same since the grand opening of the new Main Street in the summer of 1925. The Security Pacific needled him, Mr. Teesdale especially so, however, though pained to admit it, he couldn't blame the town or anyone in the town. The problem was something inside him. He craved the unchanging familiarity found within the bank walls. Over time, he felt he needed it.

***

The Town & Country, lit against the night, stood like a promise. It was always a place between where people had been and where they were going. Eddie too saw it as a gateway, a stopover before landing someplace new, someplace he'd been waiting his whole life to visit. He approached anxiously, turning over in his mind ways to mask from Mary Rose the full burden of his quirks. Perhaps Connie could help, he wondered. What if he got them together? Connie possessed ordinariness, married with two boys. She was nice, knew how to talk to people. Mary Rose was clearly close to her father. Maybe she would appreciate meeting someone in his family. Most importantly, he didn't want her to have the impression he was always alone.

When he knocked on her door, she answered unexpectedly with an upturned finger to her mouth, demanding silence. Wearing a blue wiggle dress, fit snuggly, alluringly, her face held a pained and watery gaze. Something was wrong. She hurried to the bed, kept her finger in the air. Eddie noticed the handset from the telephone was off its cradle. Mary Rose lifted the handset to her face as she sat on the bed.

"Okay, Daddy, I'm back. Someone from the motel asked if I needed towels. I was wondering why so many delays. I expected you two weeks ago. Oh, Daddy, this is positively devastating. I feel awful. And he says there's nothing to be done? Are you going to be okay if I let you go? Don't worry about me. I love you. Okay. Bye."

She hung up. She sighed before palming hands together in a gesture of prayer and rested them beneath her chin. She then paced the room, her hands remaining as they were.

He gave her some time before asking, "What's wrong?"

"Daddy discovered that my grandfather had massive secret debts."

"Meaning?"

"Meaning there's no inheritance. It's gone."

"Gosh, I'm sorry."

"Daddy's so upset."

"You won't be living here?"

"Daddy doesn't want to rush decisions. He has a little money. I told him he should come and look around."

Eddie stepped toward her. Her eyes refused to budge his way. She remained distant. He longed to resolve her problems, make her happy. What could he do?

Her figure brightened as she closed curtains on the radiant pool outside. Lamplight warmed her. She clamped her teeth onto a fingernail. All the while, she paced in bare feet on the carpet.

"Maybe it's not so bad then," Eddie suggested.

"I was hoping money would allow him to manage a little better, and I could get some freedom from him."

Watching her feet soundlessly pressing into the carpet, Eddie contemplated her words. They hung like a loose thread. He struggled with the appropriateness of prying. It was the first sign of dissatisfaction with her father. Was she yearning for a life of her own?

Eddie had hoped they could listen to *Counterspy* on the radio in her car. Instead, he told her he was tired from being out the previous night, and wished only to say again how much he enjoyed spending time with her, would welcome the opportunity to do so again sometime. He left scratching his head, disappointed, wishing he was the type of man who could make her feel better.

***

It wasn't until Thanksgiving at his sister's that Eddie met Mary Rose's father for the first time. He expected a kind and perhaps sad man, someone who'd faced hardships, and was desperately, selfishly, trying to hold onto his daughter for fear of becoming lonely. However, when Gene McCoy entered Connie's home, tension immediately filled the air. Dark circles under fast eyes, wiry, he was taut with the unpredictability of a newly caged animal. He was not at all what Eddie expected. "Nice of you to have us," he grumbled, his observations stabbing the room. What was he looking for? How could such a man have raised Mary Rose?

Eddie hoped Mary Rose's father would be impressed by his sister's conventional devotion to the holiday, her hospitality to strangers, things that could provide the necessary push to convince him to relocate. Those thoughts vanished once he set eyes on the man.

While Eddie held back, almost in another room, stunned by the sight of the person Mary Rose called daddy, Lou straightened himself, immediately sensing trouble. Warily, the two men shook hands.

"Eddie?"

"No, I'm Lou." Lou's vigilance suffered a sudden and predictable breakdown as Mary Rose stepped through the doorframe.

She wore a pearl-colored swing dress that revealed her more than Eddie had previously seen. Connie awkwardly worked her eyes over Mary Rose as well. Whether they were judgmental or sinful thoughts, it didn't matter to Eddie. He didn't like the preoccupation of others on her. Within minutes, he wanted to leave. He knew he'd made a mistake. His retreat was silence. After all, what could he possibly say?

Names were exchanged around the room, and Mary Rose offered a dainty hand to her hosts, bending down to Connie's boys, Shawn and Paul. Shawn's right eye and chin showed bruises, but as nothing was said about it, no one asked.

The day was Wednesday. Connie cooked earlier than the rest of America, because Lou, a fireman, worked on Thanksgiving. Pulling large disbelieving eyes off Mary Rose, Connie chirped, "How about putting on a record, Lou?"

Sounding like an interrogator, focusing his attention back on Mary Rose's father, and ignoring the request for music, Lou asked, "So, you're in from Los Angeles?"

"Right."

Adopting her husband's suspicious tone, Connie turned back to Mary Rose, saying, "Rich men must've thrown themselves at you in a place like that."

"Oh, you're much too kind," Mary Rose responded.

"Did they?" Connie pressed.

"What?"

"Rich men, or men in general, throw themselves at you?" Masking hostility with laughter, she exclaimed, "You look like one of those women on the noses of airplanes during the war."

"No chance men didn't ask you out," Lou added.

"Well, a few. Daddy's protective though."

Eddie hated Thanksgiving. Why so much pressure to bring people together who didn't want to be together? When he was twelve, relatives from the East Coast came for Thanksgiving and stayed a full week. He spent the whole month of November with his mother, nervously beating on carpets, polishing floors, re-painting window frames, and cooking an endless number of dishes. In the afternoon, on Thanksgiving Day, Eddie said he was taking the dog out, and ended up roaming the town for hours. He wanted the relatives to leave. They were strangers, and for him it required too much effort to pretend otherwise. When he finally did return, he walked into a house full of agitated faces. His father said, "The boy takes after his mother." It was a good insult, Eddie reflected. With a single shot, his father struck two victims.

"Wouldn't you want your daughter to date a rich man, Mr. McCoy?" Connie asked.

"I just felt she should mature first."

"She looks pretty mature," Lou joked.

"Lotsa playboys in a city like Los Angeles," Mr. McCoy stated soberly. "After a few years you get cautious."

"The table is ready," Connie announced, prompting more than one person to comment on how wonderful everything smelled.

Eddie could feel the disappointments, the harsh judgments. He detected his sister's thoughts easily from the stiffness of movements, the strain in her voice, the things unsaid she'd commonly say in more comfortable circumstances. Eddie loved his sister, he really did, but as she led them in prayer and helped everyone fill their plates, he contemplated her profound lack of ability in seeing within herself the hypocrisy of always admonishing everyone, and advising everyone and scrutinizing for vulnerabilities, when she too lived exclusively in the past, and knew little of happiness from her own choices.

"May I ask what happened to your mother?" Connie pried, directing her focus on Mary Rose.

"She died," Mr. McCoy explained. "Long time ago."

"I'm sorry to hear."

Lou threw back a hefty swig of wine. Typically he drank beer. He fidgeted in his chair before attempting to lighten the mood with mockery of his brother-in-law, "Say, Eddie, how many times you see *A Place in the Sun?*"

Not for the first time, Eddie wondered what exactly he gained pretending to like Lou. "I don't know. A few."

"Every night for two weeks, this guy," Lou laughed, jabbing a thumb in the direction of Eddie. "*A Place in the Sun.* Can you imagine? Every night."

Coming to his defense, Mary Rose said, "Eddie likes movies. What's wrong with that?"

"I tell you what," Lou went on. "If The Barstow ever goes up in flames, I don't know what this guy's gonna do. It's like these kids here. Sometimes I can't get them to turn off the stupid radio. Cowboys and masked avengers and romances; it's all so dumb. You like that stuff, Mr. McCoy?"

"No." Hunched over his food with forearms flat on the table flanking his plate, he looked like a scavenger worried about losing his turkey and potatoes. Why so greedy? Why so far removed from the manners of his daughter?

Connie smiled. "You know, I must say, in all the years Lou and I have had Thanksgiving, there've been times when Eddie has come around, times when he hasn't, but he's never once asked if he could bring guests. You two must be something special."

Compliments were given on the cooking. They talked about how fast time flies, that they couldn't believe another year was ending, Christmas was coming soon, and how different everything was from the way it used to be. Dessert was finally brought in from the kitchen and Mary Rose said, "Something tells me it wasn't the Indians who brought pies to the Pilgrims way back a hundred years ago or whenever but the other way around."

After a slight pause, Connie replied, "There were a few good things that came from Europe."

"Before spending the last year in Los Angeles," Mary Rose then added, "I was in New Mexico and saw Indians up close. They didn't look like the kind you see in picture books."

"Didn't Mr. McCoy say you've been in Los Angeles for a few years now?" Connie asked.

Mary Rose's eyes shifted quickly to her father, and then she smiled, saying, "Oh, did he? Well, that's right. I'm not the best at math."

"I may have overstated the length of our stay in Los Angeles too," Mr. McCoy explained.

Unsatisfied, Connie questioned further. "So, were the two of you in New Mexico together?"

After another fast second of eye contact between father and daughter, Mary Rose said, "Oh, no, that was before, when I was with my mother."

To Mr. McCoy, Connie pressed, "I thought you said her mother died a long time ago."

Mary Rose's father leaned back from the table, rubbed his weathered face, and said, "It's a matter of interpretation, I suppose. She's still around. I say she's dead because to me she is. See, uh, she left me for someone else. I guess it's a bit of a sore spot with me. I'd prefer to talk of something else."

"I didn't mean to pry," Connie stated simply. "I make it a point to never concern myself with other people's business."

Just as the McCoys got up to go, Eddie too left his sister's. Knowing an earful of concerns would come once Connie got a moment alone with him, he refused to give her the opportunity. Would she have some valid points? Of course, he answered himself. Something about Gene McCoy was odd. There was also something odd about the relationship with his daughter.

***

Eddie didn't care for holiday festivities. He liked that the bank was closed. Yet, he often felt empty. Nothing felt emptier than the Sunday after Thanksgiving. He hadn't seen Mary Rose, hadn't heard from her. He walked along train tracks perpendicular to Main Street. Nervousness made him leave his house, run away from routines typically performed while the rest of the town congregated at church.

The yellow valley floor offered a clean bright view, and Eddie felt strangely comforted by the distant miles and immense silence. His insignificance seemed a more measureable thing. The sky was unusual, not blue, not white or gray, but a mixture of all three. It sat there, windswept and then left alone, Eddie thought, as he looked to see if it moved.

Seeing no movement, he dropped his gaze to the earth. The stillness of earth and sky browbeat him like a conquering force. Spiritless, he faced the heavens with only hunched shoulders. Where was the train? Would it too disappoint? Stepping into the middle of the tracks, keeping his head down, he waited. Would anyone care? he pondered, looking again into the pale sky.

Facades fell, lies he'd been telling himself. How many times had he claimed a preference for being alone, or that he didn't care what other people thought about him? He convinced himself that mere minutes with Mary Rose was better than nothing, but now he had less than before, less certainty, less willingness to live his life as it had always been lived. Had precious minutes with her been enough to make up for that?

His sister telephoned—at least he felt pretty sure it was Connie—but he didn't answer. It was on Thanksgiving Day. Who else? Mary Rose didn't have his number, had not been to his house. She might have asked the switchboard operator to connect her to Mr. Howard, the assistant manager of the Security Pacific at his home, but given the holiday, she would have risked impropriety.

Eddie stepped down from the train tracks and began the long walk back to his house. The courage to end it all, it seemed, was just another pose, another lie. Instead, he would go home and clean, turn on the radio, and wait for Monday.

When the first day back after a long holiday weekend came, Mary Rose and her father made an appearance at nine forty-five. A talkative young man sat across from Eddie, having remembered him from when his mother would drag him into the Security Pacific. He couldn't believe Eddie was still there, he'd been away at an East Coast university, had taken a job near where he went to school, couldn't have found greater contentment, and couldn't get over how much Barstow remained the same.

Mr. Teesdale assisted the McCoys. She wore a fashionable pencil dress and snug sweater. Mr. McCoy was in the same clothes from five days earlier. The conversation went on for some time. Eventually, Eddie stood and smiled as the young man who knew him from years past offered a friendly goodbye.

He sat down again and pretended to busy himself while watching Mary Rose, and then Mr. Teesdale, Mary Rose and her father all stood. Mary Rose walked across the carpeted floor toward Eddie's desk. She leaned to Eddie, placed a delicate hand near his papers, and said, "Daddy found a bar where there's a pool table. He'll be there tonight. I could use some company if you're up for it."

Hours later, they were in her Chieftain, facing the pool as it glowed like a fire of cyan blue. They listened to *The Great Gildersleeve* on the radio. The program had lost something when shortened to a fifteen-minute format, Eddie believed, and mentioned so to Mary Rose. She seemed troubled, in a quiet mood. She said almost nothing for the longest time. When *Gildersleeve* ended, she clicked off the radio. What was she thinking? Eddie too felt troubled. He wanted to know why she spent time with him.

She could be with any man in the world. Why him? He'd been telling himself they had things in common, but after Thanksgiving, he was less sure. For some time she sat in the driver's seat, head down, eyes within, thinking, and then finally she faced him.

"I told you my grandfather's money is gone. You don't know how much my daddy was dependent on that money. I like your sister, Eddie, and her family. They have it nice, a cozy home, kids. They're fortunate, don't you think? Everyone should be so lucky. Many people aren't. My daddy—this is difficult, Eddie—my daddy wants to take money from the Security Pacific. A lot of money. Well, I guess he means to steal it. I don't know. I don't like the idea at all. I'm against it. Steal, that's right. I have some problems with my daddy. He is my daddy though. Oh, Eddie, why does life have to be so complicated? I never saw this coming. My daddy has reached a desperation point. That's all there is to it. Of course, I told him I could never in a million years take advantage of my friendship with you. Nevertheless, he wanted you to know. He wanted me to tell you. The way I see it, two things could happen. One is that he goes to jail. It wouldn't be the worst thing that could happen. He'd be out of my life for some time. I'd have freedom. The other possibility is that he gets away with it, and gives me some of the money. Do you understand what I'm saying? Tell me how you feel? What do you think of all this, Eddie? Won't you say something?"

Chapter Three

Mary Rose's presence in Eddie's house changed the place, made it nearly unfamiliar. All the lingering feminine touches came out, and it looked more like his folks' home than it had in years. Why were there plates on the walls? Why such a noisy floral pattern in the curtains? He'd had years to redecorate, yet everything remained untouched.

His mother had a great love of candles. Every evening, as soon as the sun fell, she'd glide through rooms, firing up an amber glow. In the living room, an oil-burning lamp hadn't been lit for years, yet Eddie's mother never let a night pass without it. Was it her Victorian upbringing in Pennsylvania she longed to get back to? In more ways than one, with its beaded shade, intricate base, and delicate glasswork, the lamp in the living room reminded Eddie of his mother. For years, Eddie felt putting a flame to it would seem an inadequate resurrection.

Mr. McCoy brought a Schlitz six-pack, a block of cheese and a box of crackers. Eddie said he'd prepare ground beef with macaroni and cheese, but Mr. McCoy told him to save it as he scooted the snacks closer to Eddie.

He cracked the top off a beer, and said, "You'll have one won't you, Eddie? Sorry I couldn't afford something a little stronger."

Eddie turned to Mary Rose and asked, "Are you going to have one?" She stood anxiously in a doorway, while he and Mr. McCoy sat at a table next to a window through which the blackness of night watched all three.

"Half a beer, maybe."

Mary Rose was quiet around her father, different, more introverted. She triggered a memory of Eddie disastrously singing in church once. He embarrassed everyone, and fell deeper within himself.

He invited Mary Rose and her father over, feigning interest in Mr. McCoy's plans, but secretly wanting time with Mary Rose, to put eyes to her, sneak glances at her voluptuousness. Her perfume came inside with her, and he wished the scent would never go away.

"I was encouraged by your invite, Eddie," Mr. McCoy said, placing an opened Schlitz before his host. "It tells me you're smart." He spoke slowly, gruffly. Eddie hadn't noticed the slight drawl at Thanksgiving. Cheeks caved in, while beneath his eyes, pale skin bulged like sacks of flesh weighted with booze and bitterness.

"You could've mentioned our little idea to the police, but you knew we would've denied it, said you was crazy," Mr. McCoy went on. "I like you, Eddie. I think we can be friends."

"Sure," Eddie muttered. Silence crept in as he realized trust was already questionable. Risks had already been taken. He sipped his beer, and then began to voice a suggestion he was working on. "I was thinking. I know you're in a bind. Your daughter told me about your father's unfortunate finances. I had an idea. You know, all day, everyday, I help people who are struggling with—"

"Do you have a knife, Eddie?"

A few seconds slipped away, and then Mr. McCoy, sensing the tension, pointed at his uncut cheese block.

"Of course," Eddie answered, hurrying to a drawer.

"You were saying," Mr. McCoy grunted, as Eddie handed him a knife.

"I was … um … I was saying I have access to information that can be helpful. I know what loans have been approved for starting new businesses next year. Perhaps I could confidentially provide you with names of people to introduce yourself to, and you could tell them you're new to the area, looking for work."

Mr. McCoy's gaunt cheeks rose over a pretend smile. "Say, that's mighty big of you, Eddie. I appreciate you doing something on my behalf. The problem is, our needs, the needs of my daughter and me, are too big to be fixed by a job working next year in a store somewheres. My father, may he rest in peace, left this world owing it a good chunk of change. Those debts could get passed on to me. Plus, I've done my bit. I've worked. And I don't got a lot to show for it. A good deal of my professional life was when times was really hard. I'm sure I don't have to tell you—"

A wrapping of knuckles at the front door startled Eddie and hushed Mr. McCoy. Rather than finish what he was saying, Mr. McCoy glared and sighed while quietly placing his beer bottle on the table. Eddie answered the unspoken question. "I don't know who it is."

"Someone's at the door," Mary Rose whispered.

Eddie hurried past her to the floral curtains. After parting them by a crack, he said, "It's my sister," and then turned back to Mary Rose and her father. "She never shows up unannounced. I'll see what she wants, tell her now's not a good time."

Outside, Eddie didn't bother with pleasantries. "What're you doing here?" he demanded to know.

Face lined with pity, Connie pointed at the Chieftain in the driveway. "Is this that woman's car?"

Angered, Eddie answered, "She's inside. So's her father." He put his hands to his hips. "What do you want?"

Careful with her volume, Connie said, "Eddie, these aren't your kind of people."

"My kind of people?"

"I was hoping we could talk."

Exasperated, stammering, Eddie managed to say, "Connie, I … even if the timing was good, I don't think this is a conversation I want to have."

"Lou and I were talking—"

"Oh, you and Lou, huh? Well, that's swell. Managing my life for me, were you?"

"Don't get upset. Just listen. I came here … Eddie, is that beer on your breath?"

"Lou drinks constantly."

"We're talking about you. You deserve better than these people."

"I deserve better? Are you blind? Mary Rose's father is probably in there asking her, 'What do you see in this guy?'"

"What does she see in you, Eddie?"

"What do you mean?"

"She's using you. It's obvious."

Eddie's chest caved. How did she know? He denied any understanding of what was happening. "Using me for what?"

"I don't know."

"But yet it's so darn obvious?"

"There's something skuzzy about them, Eddie. You must see that. Maybe you're the one who's blind."

Stepping closer, shoved by emotions beyond his control, Eddie said, "Alright, Connie, you want to know what's going on here? She makes me feel good." His voice quivered as he continued, choked by his confession. "Is that too complicated a thing for you to understand? She makes me feel good. I don't know if I've ever felt good before. You're probably right. I'm sure you are. You're always right, Connie. Maybe she's using me. Maybe I've reached a point where I don't care."

"Eddie, you have me and Lou—"

"Oh, yeah? Lou? Let me ask you something. What happened to Shawn's face?"

The question silenced Connie's concerns, and after her face fell, she couldn't look at her brother again.

"That's what I thought. I got to get back inside. I don't want to be rude."

Shutting the door on his sister, he shook his head and waved away the drama his guests might have overheard. "It's nothing. It's fine."

"You're house sure is clean." Mary Rose smiled as she complimented him. Was she trying to assuage his angst, make him feel better? Was the house too clean? Again he was reminded of things his father would say to his mother.

"You and your sister are close," Mr. McCoy said when Eddie re-entered the kitchen.

"Yeah, I guess." He sat. "I don't know."

"Have a cracker and some cheese."

"Okay."

"She upset?"

Eddie got a different knife, not wanting to use the same one as Mr. McCoy. "She's always telling me what to do. It's nothing."

From the adjacent room, Mary Rose shouted, "Mind if I put on a record?"

Eddie never played music. He'd let years go by without sifting through the albums stacked in a corner. He mostly listened to programs voiced by movie stars. What were the hits? Elvis?

"If you find something you like, sure," he replied. The Schlitz helped. He slumped in his chair, munching on Mr. McCoy's snacks.

When the music started, he was surprised by his immediate familiarity with it. So many years had passed. Xavier Cugat put a samba on the dance floors called *Brazil* back in 1943 or '44, he wasn't really sure. The sounds of trumpets filled the house, and through the door to the next room, Eddie caught glimpses of Mary Rose dancing. She reminded him of Dorothy Malone in *Written on the Wind*.

Hadn't he deserved some kind of chance at happiness? Was this the gateway needed to earn something resembling confidence, an existence absent so many fears?

There was no right decision, Eddie told himself; there was only what came next. Could he really condemn himself to a life without change?

"Ever been to Brazil?" Mr. McCoy asked. "I spent some time in São Paulo. That's a city that goes on forever, and not just across the land, but high up into the clouds too. Beautiful place."

Intrigued, eyes falling within, Eddie murmured, "Sounds great."

"I been all over. Rio, Santiago. I been to Europe. Lisbon, Barcelona. I was in Barcelona just after the civil war. There was still a lot of tension in the air, whispers of a political underground anxious for action. I spent a night outside the city with gypsies. Beautiful place. Barcelona. The streetlamps alone will make you cry.

You should see the world, Eddie. Don't you ever want to make love to beautiful women from other countries? Don't you ever get tired of hearing the same jokes from customers day in, day out? Ever get tired of being a banker? Tired of Barstow? You can start life again, Eddie. You can change."

Big Fat Clem, the town joker, had a standard line. "Not much chance of snow in Barstow. And that there's the one thing I can take to the bank." Getting his weekly laugh, Clem would tug on his suspenders, tip his hat, and waddle off. Sally the Screamer always came into the bank on Wednesdays. Her two boys were the worst behaved in Barstow. "Keep your mitts outta the garbage!" she'd yell, and sure enough, every week, one of her boys would dunk his head in the trash. Sally would react as if it couldn't have been predicted. She'd scream and slap the boy hard enough to rattle teeth. And there was Jeremiah Richter. He had a neighbor, Heidi, who was a schoolteacher. Something grew in Heidi's brain and she died a slow death. For many months afterwards, Jeremiah would come into the bank, shake his head, and say, "Oh, poor Heidi ... just terrible." It went on for months. When nearly a year later Jeremiah was still coming into the bank, expressing the same devastation, Eddie began to wonder about him. Would he be forever shocked? Had God's promise of eventual death escaped his comprehension somehow? He was aware that he would die too sometime, right?

"It worries me," Eddie uttered simply, after much thought.

"I'll be honest. Can I be honest? I've done this before. I've done it many times. Never been caught."

Surprised, Eddie raised his eyes to Mr. McCoy, quickly wondering why he was surprised, and then agonized over the temptations presented. "How would you, you know, how would you do it?"

"I tell Teesdale I found the house I want, I'm just waiting for my money to come from my father's estate. Obviously, nothing is said about any debts. If he thinks I'm flush, he's less likely to be suspicious. Once the job is done, we linger, we wait, tell Teesdale there's some delay with the funds, some lawyer causing problems. Eventually, I tell him I have to get back to Los Angeles to clear up some mess to do with the estate. At that point, I'm gone from Barstow forever. Anyone tracks me down, sees I'm spending a little dough, will assume it came from my father as opposed to the bank. As long as no one looks too closely, it's a story that makes sense."

"Except you expressed interest in a house, and then didn't buy it."

"Happens all the time."

"Your daughter said it would happen overnight."

"That's right. We're not the gun-waving, mask-wearing type. We'll get into the safe. We're also not greedy. We're not taking everything. For a while it might not even look like anything's gone, as if a robbery never even occurred."

"Technically, it's not a robbery."

"What're you saying?"

"It's a burglary. It would be a robbery if there were people there, if you stole from people while they were present. A burglary is breaking and entering and stealing with no one there. It's a small thing, just a detail. No big deal."

"Thank you very much for that explanation, Eddie."

"It's not important but … anyway, how do you … how do you get into the safe?"

"Don't worry about it."

"I don't have the combination. Mr. Teesdale does, plus someone at headquarters. We're a branch, remember? I can't get you into the safe."

"Don't worry."

"What if we get caught?"

"Eddie, you're not robbing the bank. You're making a mistake with the front door that probably won't even get noticed. No one will be able to accuse you of a crime."

Eddie gulped the last of his beer, wiped his upper lip with a shirtsleeve, as Mr. McCoy kindly gave him another. "Yet, I would be. Committing a crime. I've never committed a crime before. Never so much as stole a candy bar. It could come out. It's possible that all would be revealed. What then?"

"It's not gonna happen. But if it does, you go to jail for a few years, maybe only a couple of years. Not a big deal, not like killing someone. Aren't you in jail already sitting there at that bank, day after day? Consider the freedom you're giving up there."

"It's not the same thing. I could always leave the bank—"

"But you don't."

"I could though. I can if I want to. I could go from working at the bank to some other job. Much harder to go from being a jailbird to some other job."

"Look, Eddie, I know you're fond of my daughter. If not for me, do it for her."

"And then what?"

"What do you mean?"

"Afterwards? What do I do?"

"You get outta here. I'm going to Peru. You can do whatever you want. You should wait a while though, maybe a year. You and Mary Rose can go someplace together if you want. She likes you. Pick a spot and go. Live a little. But you shouldn't stay here. Not in Barstow. Even though the bank would cover its loss—I'm sure they're insured for such things—you still might feel you're living off your neighbors' earnings. You don't need a guilty conscious creeping into your gut. Go someplace else. Forget about this town. You'll be surprised how fast they'll forget about you."

"I'd probably want to stay."

"Why?"

"This is my house. I grew up here."

"So?"

"I just don't think I'd want to move into a new house. My stuff is here. It's what I know. I'm comfortable. I like it."

"Yeah, it's nice, of course. But I think you should go. It'll toughen you up besides giving you something new to see. See the world, Eddie. It's waiting for you."

"I just can't imagine leaving this house. I don't think I could do it."

"Then why do this job?"

"What do you mean?"

"What am I offering you?"

"Well," Eddie paused, "Mr. Teesdale has never been very kind to me. I wouldn't mind if he suffered a little, I guess."

Mr. McCoy squinted skeptically. "Sure this is what you want to do?"

"I think so."

"And afterwards, everything goes well, you're not leaving this house?"

"No."

"It's up to you. Stay if you have to. Is it settled then? You're in?"

"I don't know."

"Do the smart thing, Eddie. Listen, I have a friend who'll help us with the safe. He'll arrive the night of the job and leave the night of the job. He'll take all the money we walk with, my share, your share and his share. What's ours will come to us later. That way anyone gets suspicious, we're holding nothing. You in?"

"I just don't know. It sounds good. Except for the jail part. I just … I have to think about it."

***

After the latest Saturday morning shift with Sue and Lynette, Eddie faced a new weekend. Alone during the last few days, he'd watched all his evening programs, including *Dragnet* and *The Bob Cummings Show*. Movies at The Barstow lacked their usual pull. He'd not heard from his sister again, nor Mary Rose or her father.

He retrieved a cardboard Santa Claus from his garage then marched around his house toward his front door with it. Christmas came with mixed feelings. Decorations and carolers warmed his heart. Happiness from others spilled into his house in small doses. Sometimes the characters he lived vicariously through on radio and TV reminded him of the season's charm. Mostly, however, Christmas reinforced Eddie's loneliness.

Staring at Santa's rosy cheeks and jolly smile, he considered how he'd always been a good boy. At times, thoughts were harsh toward those around him. He had lustful thoughts about Mary Rose; he couldn't help it. Yet in action, he'd always been well behaved. Rewards were promised for such conduct. Where were they? Where were the rewards he so richly deserved? Had there been any pay-off he could point to?

For a while, he convinced himself Mary Rose had arrived as a divine gift. He found happiness believing a heavenly hand nudged her his way. Her presence transformed him, and he relished the transformation.

She said she wanted to get away from her father, she didn't agree with him about some things, even insinuated she wouldn't mind if he went to jail. Could it be that Mary Rose did possess a fondness for Eddie? Maybe her interest in him had nothing to do with his position at the bank. Maybe it truly was something more. Could he not return to his previous beliefs about her? Why not? He had faith in God, yet doubted. Could he not have faith in Mary Rose? Given his improved frame of mind during the last five weeks, it was painful to imagine life without her.

After fastening Santa to his front door, Eddie thought about going to the market for some beer. He never drank beer but liked it the other day. The beer made him feel closer to normal for a few moments. He wouldn't drink a beer with dinner, but maybe after. Should he get some? What if Ethel, who worked at the market and always said hello, noticed the unusual purchase? How would he explain that he was suddenly a beer drinker?

That Ethel might question him about six bottles of beer was, as Eddie thought about it, perhaps a sensible argument for robbing the bank. Who would suspect him? He lived a simple life, loyal to the bank, had no debts. To most of Barstow, he was like a dog on the sidewalk, passed by, rarely given a nickel's worth of attention.

Mr. McCoy said Eddie wouldn't have to be anywhere near the bank on the night of the heist. He could hand the key to them after work, and they could bring it back early the next morning or, if Eddie preferred, he could swing by the bank in the middle of the night, unlock the door, and go home. Easy, he figured. In spite of this, a worry nagged at him. What if Mr. McCoy planned to leave evidence at the bank that indicated Eddie was the culprit, perhaps even the sole culprit? Mr. McCoy was not trustworthy, of that he was certain. In this moment, Eddie found the clarity eluding him, making him feel insecure about getting involved with such a plan. If he were to partake in the heist, even as a tiny contributor, he would have to assume some control over the entire affair. That meant keeping eyeballs firmly locked on all players. In pictures, it was always the little guy convinced he had almost no involvement in a crime that the others would pin the whole thing on. Eddie had a sense of this from the beginning. Only now had he been able to articulate it in his mind. There were no minor roles when staging a bank heist.

By evening, Eddie had pretty much made up his mind. He went back and forth again and again before deciding resentment of his past trumped confidence in his future. The cost would be one entire night off from his routine, and he'd effectively crossed that line recently with Mary Rose, so he was certainly capable of such a thing. In addition, the bank would lose a little money. As money wasn't his key motivator, he would tell Mr. McCoy to reduce his share and leave the rest with the bank to make it less conspicuous. He would also insist Mary Rose not be there. If anything went wrong, he didn't want her getting into trouble.

He imagined his life afterwards. Mary Rose's father would be gone. She said she could get some freedom from him. Would she stay at Eddie's house? How would she react to his invite? He spoke with a voice like Bogart as police rolled to his curb and he said to her, "Just keep your pretty head clear. Everything'll be alright." Once police left, outwitted by his evasiveness, Mary Rose went into his bedroom, slipped out of her clothes, and asked him to enter. Could life be something like that?

The next day, Sunday, he went to the Town & Country and told Mr. McCoy to set the date. All his conditions were met without hesitation. It was a book closing, his life thus far. From now on, he'd be starting a new one. It was a moment of liberation, he told himself. He had to think of it that way. Doubts and guilt would get the better of him otherwise.

That night, after dinner, Mr. McCoy stood calmly at his door, and said, "An hour past midnight. Wednesday. To be clear, that's really Thursday morning. Got it? We'll pick you up here."

The following three days were long, nervous, nail-biting days. Eddie had no appetite. He couldn't sleep. At the bank, a plastic nativity scene stood in haughty somber-faced judgment. Hours before the big moment, he grabbed the telephone, wanting to tell Mr. McCoy that Mr. Teesdale was sick, home, and suspicion might fall on Eddie if they pulled it off with the bank manager absent. Eddie hung up the telephone before dialing. He couldn't bring himself to lie, as trust was already questionable. Plus, he thought it better to get the job done. Why prolong the handwringing and agonizing? Thursday, December 12, seemed as good a time as any. Maybe it would be easy. Maybe everything would run smoothly. Maybe the dread he felt was nothing more than the voices of his mother and father, devastated, screaming at him for involving himself in a crime.

Chapter Four

Eddie went outside through the back door, checked the lock the usual number of times, and then considered the irony of his task. Ambivalence remained, twisting him into a knot. The night's blackness struck him as a chill in his clothing. He went to the front of the house. All lights were off. He walked one block, and waited. He lowered his hat and squeezed his eyes shut for a moment. This is terrible, he thought, wrong and irreversible. A secret would be launched, one which confession could offer no Earthly salvation. From here forward, he would be hiding something, pretending to be someone good. He could never be himself again. He could never allow anyone to truly get to know him.

From shadows, an engine roared to life. The sight of an automobile with blackened headlights stretched his spine. Would they kill him and take the key? Presumably, the safecracker was already on board. They would soon have everything they'd need. They could toss his corpse in a trunk and be done with him.

He'd seen too many pictures, he reminded himself, read too many pulps. Mary Rose was sweet. An evil home could never have reared such beauty.

The car crept very near. The driver's side window was down. "Get in," Mr. McCoy said from behind the wheel.

Leaning into the window, Eddie saw Mary Rose in the passenger seat. Like a statue, she faced the windshield and the dark road beyond. Eddie knew, given his insistence that she not participate, this was the first of what would be numerous betrayals. Nevertheless, he steeled himself and got into the back of Mr. McCoy's Plymouth.

They cruised the same streets Eddie bicycled as a boy. The weight of such nostalgia, the confrontation with his younger self, struck with the force of a hatchet to his already frayed nerves. Nearing Main Street, Mr. McCoy's headlights suddenly blazed, adding a pair of probing beams to the streetlamps and stars. Yet the darkness remained. It was a ghost town, not a resident in sight. The townspeople were decent, hardworking, and therefore sleeping in their beds where they should be, never thinking there might be a need to protect their meaty bones from scavengers. With a sigh, Eddie hung his head, closed his eyes, and moments later felt the Plymouth make a turn.

Mr. McCoy's headlights swept the rear of the Security Pacific. A Roadmaster Riviera, prized possession of Mr. Teesdale, always reflected a dazzling white sunshine during business hours in the space right by the back door. The lot was empty now, and the dark emptiness made an impression on Eddie.

"Where's Mr. Green?" Mary Rose wondered aloud.

"Must not be here yet," her father responded before killing his narrow lights.

"What do we do?"

"We wait."

"What if he doesn't show?" Eddie asked, although his concern was never answered.

Ignored by Mr. McCoy, Eddie was thrown a fast smile by Mary Rose. It might have been a reassuring smile, but he couldn't tell. Eddie had no idea what she was thinking. Nevertheless, he looked at her repeatedly as if her silent beauty spoke to his anxieties, and told him everything would work out just fine.

They waited. Would there be enough time? Eddie wondered. How fast was Mr. McCoy's friend at breaking into a safe? In five hours, sunlight would discover them. In four and a half, neighbors would start walking dogs. As minutes passed, Eddie rationalized his involvement. How much snickering had he endured? How much condescension from Mr. Teesdale? How many customers accused him of mistakes only to later discover errors in their own bookkeeping? Had any of them apologized? For being a little different, the whole town hated him.

"What time is it?" Mary Rose asked.

"It's late," Mr. McCoy said, and then looked at his watch. "Ten minutes before two."

"Maybe we should do this another time," Eddie suggested.

"Don't get jittery," Mr. McCoy grumbled.

"He's an hour late."

"You're free to walk home if you like. Leave us the key, we'll drop it off in the morning."

Eddie simmered for a moment, his nerves rattling to the point where he didn't know how much longer he could take it, and then he said, "Well, based on your extensive experience with this kind of thing, how much time do you foresee it taking to accomplish this job?"

"Mr. Green is a pro. Don't worry."

"The safe is old," Eddie added.

"This time tomorrow you'll be sleeping like a baby."

Forty minutes later, lights speared Main Street. Mr. Green had arrived, they thought, until the automobile rolled past without stopping. It was excruciating. All signs were ominous. Eddie knew he'd made a mistake. Would he go to jail? How could he turn this around? He knew things, he reminded himself. Unless he could convince Mr. McCoy to abandon ship, he'd need to remain committed.

At five minutes past three, another set of lights approached. "That's him. Got to be," Mr. McCoy said. Sure enough, the vehicle parked. "Green's not his name, Eddie, but that's what you'll call him. Just like my name's not really McCoy. You don't know my name, see, just like you don't know my daughter's. Truth is, you know very little about us. I'm telling you this in case things hit a snag, and you get some funny ideas about flapping your gums. You'll look like an idiot. They might just think you're making things up. Understand?"

Nearly freak show thin, Mr. Green stood from his car, an old Coupe, put a small fist to his mouth, and coughed. Gray hair hung over his ears, uncombed, straggly, fitting with his buzzard-stooped posture.

"Let's get to work," Mr. McCoy said, exiting the Plymouth. Eddie and Mary Rose followed.

Mr. Green struck a match, and lit a cigarette, throwing orange light on his downward cast face. After a deep drag, he exhaled a long plume of smoke that disappeared into the night like a speeding train.

Nearing his cohort, Mr. McCoy snapped, "You're late."

Rather than reply, Mr. Green raised his eyes to Eddie and wouldn't let go. He scrutinized, unreadable, while Eddie stood silent. Though not terribly intimidating, the man was so unapproachable, Eddie didn't even offer a greeting. Peculiar, not what he expected, Eddie thought of Mr. Green, not much of a tough guy. Nevertheless, there was a tragic recklessness in the man's eyes, a cold indifference to everything around him.

"What happened?" Mr. McCoy demanded to know.

"Flat tire," Mr. Green stated without a hint of it having been a nuisance, keeping his eyes on Eddie, and then adding, "It's a party?"

"He works here. He's getting us inside."

"At what cost?"

Mr. McCoy looked at Eddie and said, "Why don't you go around front, get us in."

Such surreal circumstances inside the bank's darkened and vacant interior prompted Eddie's seventeen-year career to rush his mind. So many unmemorable days, he thought, the sad ransom paid to his anxious nature. He'd never been inside the Security Pacific at three in the morning. The emptiness and gloominess was more than he'd imagined. He'd be back in a few hours, duty-bound to the same tired routine, but for how long could he stay? For how long could he protect such a secret? Would there be enough money for him to leave?

With only moonlight through the windows, he navigated his way across the carpeted floor before entering a short hallway. He unlocked a storage room past Mr. Teesdale's office. Why had Mr. Green seemed surprised by Eddie's presence? Inside, flanked by stacks of boxes, was a back door. Eddie rubbed a face knotted with a thousand fears. Just do the simple things you were asked to do, he told himself.

After a deep breath, he opened the back door, keeping the storage room dark so no light could spill from within. The men entered, followed by Mary Rose. Her shoulder touched him. He could smell perfume, the scent mixed with Mr. Green's smoke trail.

"We're following your lead, Eddie." Mr. McCoy's voice sounded lower. Was it the darkness playing tricks? He spoke with something resembling a cowboy's whisky-throated richness. He'd robbed banks in the past. Had he killed anyone?

The safe was in the accounting room, where Eddie spent Saturdays with Lynette and Sue. Guiding his cohorts through the darkness, Eddie considered that Mr. Teesdale always said the safe contained no more than seventy-five thousand dollars but Eddie thought the figure low, and once calculated that if every customer withdrew fourteen dollars at the same time they would be completely out of cash, everything would be gone. What if Mr. Teesdale wasn't telling the truth? What if the safe contained more than seventy-five thousand dollars?

Eddie shut the door before flipping a light switch. The accounting room had no windows. Eddie's first good look at the skeletal Mr. Green was unsettling. Cold indifference, inspected closer, looked more like his father when caught staring beyond his final days. Was Mr. Green sick?

"It's half past three," Mr. McCoy said.

"I'm tired," Mary Rose chimed in, complaining.

"That's not my point," her father snapped. "We've little time."

"I do this alone," Mr. Green said.

"You want us to go somewheres?"

There was tension between them. Mr. Green nodded at Mr. McCoy. Had they only just now met? With the back of a hand, Mr. McCoy wiped above his lips. He paced the room, and then said, "How do I know you won't pocket a few extra bills?"

Mr. Green said nothing. Meeting the question with only silence worked up Mr. McCoy further. Finally, after three or four minutes wasted, Mr. McCoy pointed at Eddie with a thumb and said, "We'll go but he stays. He's quiet as a church mouse."

The old man's gray and yellow eyes had something of Methuselah in them. They probed Eddie, making him uncomfortable. Eddie felt himself read like a slim paperback. "Absolute silence," Mr. Green finally said. Though spoken with a frail rasp, the two words had an impact.

"Come get us when you're in," Mr. McCoy insisted before flipping the light off. He opened the door. Pale moonlight hit him as he shuffled into the customer area with Mary Rose at his back.

Once the door shut again, and the McCoys were gone, Eddie turned the light back on. Mr. Green knelt to the safe. It was a Diebold from a decade back, sturdy and mean-looking. A tornado would be enraged by its immovability. Mr. Green, however, seemed unimpressed. He flattened a palm on the square metal door with one hand, and with the other began spinning the dial clockwise and counter-clockwise. He listened intently like a doctor to a heartbeat. Counter clockwise some more and then clockwise, he continued on and on.

Eddie looked at his watch. It was ten minutes till four. How much time would this take? In an hour and a half, Main Street would see headlights. Automobiles and foot-traffic would swoop in. The Continental would be serving breakfasts by six.

He thought about making love to Mary Rose. He had little experience in the area, just an awkward night in the summer of 1934 with Hortense Trevor, and another with a grieving widow named Marie MacDonald during the war. Once with Mary Rose, even a kiss and a light touch with his hands, would be amazing. How could any man think clearly around her?

Mr. Green pulled a short pencil and slip of paper from a pocket. He wrote down a number. Eddie could see over the narrow shoulders. With the number on the paper, Mr. Green resumed dialing and listening. Three times he did this, before handing the slip of paper to Eddie. "Might as well do something."

"What?"

"Read the numbers when I tell you," Mr. Green instructed him. He wiggled the fingers of his right hand. He then delicately placed them back on the dial, and whispered, "First number."

"Fifty-eight."

Eddie watched the insect-thin old man whirl the dial four times counter clockwise before stopping at fifty-eight. Was Eddie really doing this? Reality slipped between his ears, offering clarity as if his were the deeds of someone else. His heart sank like an anchor on a great ship.

"Second number."

"Thirty-two."

Mr. Green rotated the dial three times clockwise, stopping then at thirty-two.

"Third number."

"Twenty-nine."

Twice counter-clockwise the dial went before landing on twenty-nine. Without hesitation, Mr. Green grabbed the lever and thrust downward. The square metal door didn't budge. Calmly, Mr. Green asked, "Fifty-eight, thirty-two, twenty-nine?"

"That's right."

Again, Mr. Green attempted the same configurations without success. On the third try, he didn't ask Eddie for the numbers. He knew them. Without hesitation, he persisted with the combination.

It's over, Eddie thought with some relief, and then fretted over Mr. McCoy's response. He'd be stubborn. He'd dig his heels in. He wouldn't admit time had run out. At the very least, he'd want to come back, but Eddie felt this failure was an omen. He was done. He'd tried, and it didn't work. Could he get out of it? Would they trust his promise of silence? Most likely not, he answered himself.

After spinning to the same numbers, Mr. Green pulled on the lever a fifth or sixth time—Eddie had lost count—and amazingly, like the be-all-end-all of a Houdini act, the safe door opened. Inside were rows of neatly piled stacks of cash. Eddie felt a rush of excitement. His chest broadened with the pounding of his newly invigorated heart. Waiting for Mr. Green to speak, he licked dry lips and wished the world could know what its aggressions had wrought. The Security Pacific practically owed Eddie a few stacks of moolah for all the abuse and boredom he'd suffered.

On the other hand, Eddie wasn't averse to being cruel. He'd tossed scornful looks, lashed out with insults. What am I doing? He considered uncomfortably. Did the people of Barstow deserve to have their hard-earned money stolen?

"Count it," rasped Mr. Green.

"You want me to count it?"

"Make it fast."

Eddie kneeled and pulled stacks from the Diebold. He could tell there wasn't seventy-five thousand dollars. Was there a smaller safe elsewhere Eddie didn't know about, some secret stash with more? The bills were in bundles of hundreds, fifties and twenties. In less than ten minutes, he'd added up a total of forty-eight thousand dollars.

"Get Gene, tell him what we're looking at," Mr. Green said, when told of the low amount.

"He'll be upset."

"There's little time."

Hustling through the darkened bank to Mr. McCoy, Eddie thought of proposing the idea that they leave the cash in the safe, remove all traces of having been there, maybe he could pay closer attention to amounts coming and going, and they could make a bigger score some other time. Every detail had become a fiasco. All signs pointed toward disaster. Why risk so much for so little?

Eddie barely saw Mary Rose and her father before Mr. McCoy shot through the door Eddie opened. Mr. McCoy focused only on what little trust he had in Mr. Green being left alone. Anxious to unburden bad news, and gauge her reaction, Eddie said to Mary Rose, "There's not that much money."

She had no reaction, remaining as silent as she had been all night. Eddie walked with her, side by side, saying nothing further. When they returned to the accounting room, Mr. McCoy, having obviously been informed, fired off an enraged look at Eddie.

"I wish there was a million dollars," he said defensively, as Mr. McCoy glared. "But there's not. That's just the way it is. It's not my fault. There's no reason to be upset with me."

"Forty-eight grand." Spitting mad, Mr. McCoy turned and paced. Eddie thought he might punch a wall. "How often does Teesdale get in here?"

Eddie shrugged. "Whenever there's a large withdrawal. All the time."

By Eddie's watch, only an hour and fifteen minutes remained before early risers would be turning their eyes toward Main Street. He was tempted to walk away, deny any involvement. He had no unlawful history. Would people believe him? Probably not, he admitted. However, more than anything else, what stopped him was realizing he'd changed since meeting Mary Rose. His expectations on life had changed. He had feelings beyond hurt and petty frustrations, and he didn't want them to go away.

"The amount is what it is," Mr. Green interjected.

Mr. McCoy stared at Mr. Green for a long time. Finally, quietly, he said, "How about I check your pockets?"

"If you like."

Mr. McCoy didn't move. He didn't check the pockets. He stewed, looked around without going anywhere. Eyes full of suspicion examined Eddie twice, as he went on thinking, contemplating his best angle. "Okay," he said, arriving at a decision. "We take it all. And we leave this town, all of us."

Clawing his forehead, surprised, Eddie said, "That's not what you … you said we'd leave some, enough to where this might go unnoticed for a while."

"It's a paltry forty-eight thousand dollars," Mr. McCoy argued with Eddie. "You want to leave enough to where no one notices anything missing and split the take three ways? You want we should each take a nickel?"

"We'd still have to sit on it," Mr. Green said agreeably. "No floating it around."

Confidently, Mr. McCoy replied, "I don't have a problem with that."

"Mr. McCoy, look, the recklessness has gone far enough," Eddie insisted. "I'm done. The plan you promised hasn't been followed at all. Taking everything will get noticed right away. A burglary at the Security Pacific, everything gone, will be the biggest news in Barstow history. You'll be a suspect. Everyone knows you're new, visiting. You might as well give yourself up now."

"We're not sticking around."

"But you said—"

"Change of plans, Eddie. Success requires adaptability. We all scram. And you're coming with us."

"I'm going home."

"Home no longer exists." Mr. McCoy brought his ragged face to Eddie, raising the sacks of flesh under his eyes into a squint. "I'm sorry. You should've thought this through more carefully."

Mr. McCoy's implication raced through a maze of fears before settling firmly in Eddie's brain. With Eddie gone, permanently removed—that's what he was alluding to, right?—Mr. McCoy's wallet not only fattened considerably, but his chances of escape were better. It was just a matter of timing. He'd probably kill Eddie in the desert where it would be easy to make him disappear. Eddie imagined people forever wondering what happened to him and never finding out. He blamed himself. He'd been a fool. After forty years as the most cautious man on the planet, he'd taken one risk, and lost everything.

"Be nice," Mary Rose said, trying to soften her father's hardened tone.

A moment later, Mr. McCoy noticeably brightened, not in response to Mary Rose's admonition but instead from the sight of Mr. Green raking bundles of cash into brown paper sacks. "Be nice?" he barked. "Ha! You be nice, baby." Whirling from the emptied safe, he cupped his hands to the sides of Mary Rose's face and kissed her lips.

The kiss was long. She held his wrists, struggling, and then shoved him off, crying, "Gene! Stop it!"

Dismissing her, Mr. McCoy shouted, "Who cares what he knows now. We're done here. Let's hit the road."

The next seconds passed slowly. She turned her back, unable to look at Eddie. Ill equipped to grasp the depth of such deception in an instant, the shock hit like a series of attacks when in fact it was only one. Inside, Eddie quaked. The pain from a thousand foils pierced his organs, neatly and without rush because there really were no weapons, just the gradual revelation that the one who had all his love betrayed him.

"You going to cry?" Mr. McCoy smirked. He lightly slapped the fat of Eddie's face twice. "Go ahead, Eddie, have a good cry."

Eddie shook, machine gunned with heartbreak and humiliation. Weakened by everything coming at him so quickly, he felt he might collapse.

Mary Rose pivoted back, quivering with emotion, unleashing a surprising temper. "Don't be such an asshole!"

The smirk didn't budge. "Such language," he said mockingly.

"Am I missing something?" Mr. Green inquired.

"This sap somehow got the wrong idea about my Mary Rose and me."

"Everything understood now? We don't need short fuses."

Mr. McCoy neared Eddie again, asking, "Everything understood?" Eyes lost within, Eddie didn't respond. Mr. McCoy pinched his cheek, toying with him. "Good to go, Eddie?" Eddie pushed the hand away, and without looking at Mr. McCoy, tapped his thick glasses back up to the top of his nose, and nodded.

***

Only two bags were needed for the cash. With the Diebold shut and locked, Mr. Green carried both. Eddie wondered if this would be the last he'd see of the accounting room. Good-bye, Lynette and Sue, he said silently, and then fretted over what they would think. Surely, they'd be shocked. They'd shake their heads and pinpoint with certainty the mistakes Eddie made to lead him so far astray. The whole town would despise him, everybody he'd ever known.

By Mr. McCoy's hand, the light went dark, and he said, "I have to put the Plymouth somewheres." In the customer area, they were shadow people, given a hint of dimension by a generous moon. To Mr. Green, he added, "You brought a few containers of gasoline like we talked about?"

"Couple of days' worth."

Eddie didn't know what they were talking about, and didn't care. Despite the futility of such thoughts, he tried to find a way to quickly turn all this horror around and show up for work. He reconsidered his old life, realizing it could've been worse. He wished he could start over. What's done is done, he reminded himself. His story was a tragic one: he went from fear to failure to nothing. Death now stood at arm's length, and he was ready to grab hold, get it over with. He wanted to tell Mr. McCoy, but he couldn't bring himself to utter a single word.

"We told some people we're from Los Angeles. We should head someplace else."

"We'll cross into Arizona."

The time was four-thirty. Maybe a produce truck would roll by and spot them, Eddie hoped, anything to put them on a different course. They passed Mr. Teesdale's office, shuffling into the storage room. Before leaving the building forever, Eddie hit upon an idea. With no time to think it through, he said, "I should check the lock at the front. Might be mid-day or later before Mr. Teesdale opens the safe, but everybody will be alerted if the front door's not locked."

With no traces of friendliness remaining, Mr. McCoy said, "If you think you're going to run into the street screaming for help, think again."

"I don't know if I locked it when I came in."

"Won't someone find it odd when you don't show up in the morning?"

"I can call in sick. Might buy some time."

To Mary Rose, Mr. McCoy sighed and grumbled impatiently, "You go out with Green. I'll follow Eddie. We'll be right out."

Returned to the customer area—he and Mr. McCoy alone this time—Eddie wondered if a knife or a gun was concealed. Wouldn't Mr. McCoy carry a weapon? It seemed sensible given the unpredictable nature of a bank heist. What would it feel like getting gunned down? Eddie wondered. Would death be instant? Why was Mary Rose upset with Mr. McCoy? Was it possible she had feelings for Eddie despite her lies? Before getting to the door, Mr. McCoy said, "Why don't you rattle it a few extra times for me while you're at it? I've seen the way you get."

Abruptly, Eddie turned. He marched to the teller stations, picking up speed as he went, saying, "Might be cash left from the end of the day."

Mr. McCoy quickly lunged after him. Anticipating a chase, Eddie ran to a station, arriving first by a second or two. He bent down beneath a high desk. Seized roughly and twisted around, Eddie saw a balled fist, cocked and aimed for his face. He felt it coming, anticipated the horrendous blow, but instead heard Mr. McCoy cry out, "What did you just do?"

"I triggered the alarm," Eddie lied.

The fist pummeled him, breaking his glasses; it felt harder than muscles and bones. His head jerked back. His neck took the beating almost as hard as his eye. More savage cracks landed, driving downward, as Eddie had fallen forward. It was the same fist, this time hammering into his left ear. A shriek escaped. He tried collapsing to the carpet, but Mr. McCoy held onto him.

"Where is it?" Mr. McCoy roared. "Show it to me!"

Dazed and breathless, reeling from the punches, Eddie raised a shaking hand and pointed at an alarm. "It's knee-triggered. Press it and it goes right to the police station," he said, between desperate gasps for air. "I'm not going anywhere with you."

Furious, Mr. McCoy dropped Eddie. He kicked him in the back, and snarled, "Son of a bitch." He stomped on him repeatedly until he too lost breath and fell into a wall, winded.

Unable to cope with reality, Eddie continued to believe something might save him. Pressing the alarm would've brought the police right to him. With more time, maybe he could still get out of this, he reasoned. But if it was all over for him, if the end had come, he wanted his body near the alarm, so that the impression would be that he was trying to prevent his customers from losing their money. He told himself people might think he was kidnapped and brought to the bank in the night against his will.

Feeling sharp pains and a pounding in his head, Eddie rolled onto his back, choked on blood draining from his nose, and sensed more than saw Mr. McCoy hovering above. "Not going with you," Eddie managed to repeat.

"Get up."

"Don't you have a gun like a real villain? Why don't you show some guts and just take me out now?"

A shoe punched his stomach, stomping three times, causing Eddie to roll over and vomit. Crouched, Mr. McCoy grabbed an arm and hoisted Eddie up onto his knees. He dragged him off, seething, "Get on your feet, son of a bitch."

"Wait," Eddie begged. A second gurgle of puke shot from deep within. Mr. McCoy dropped Eddie into a hacking and sobbing mess. Worse still, Eddie experienced a spinning sensation and blinding flashes. With tears gushing, he muttered, "Just leave me."

"I can't, you dumb bastard. You're coming with me."

"I don't want to go," Eddie cried, his voice punching and stalling, crippled with emotion. "I want to die," he shouted. "I don't want to live."

The stitch of his jacket ripped. He couldn't get on his feet if he wanted to; the bank had become an amusement park ride, throwing him round and round. There was a Christmas tree with moon-sparkled garland and glass ornaments. In the storage room, he crashed into boxes. How'd he get in the storage room? A hand clawed into the back of his neck. Another hand had his left arm, shoving him onward.

A door blew open. Eddie sucked in night air. The pavement hurt his knees. He fell forward, pressing concrete to his cheek. Salt from tears slipped into his mouth, mixing with the taste of puke and blood. Mary Rose stood somewhere, not far, shouting at Gene. Where was she? What was she saying? Her voice sounded so small, like Eddie was underwater, in a pool, and she was angry with someone up above.

***

They left Mr. McCoy's Plymouth at Harold B. Seton Elementary. Mr. Green had followed with Eddie in the back. Before driving away from the school, all four of them together, Eddie marveled at how much of his life had been observed by the windows of that school. Had those same windows now seen it end? Eddie wished it to be so. For him, the end couldn't come fast enough.

Mary Rose sat in the passenger seat up front, Mr. McCoy in the back with Eddie. Brown sacks of groceries were between them. Some revealed bread and cereal, while others had been clenched shut, including the two sacks of cash inconspicuous among the bunch. It seemed they thought of everything.

Aside from dizziness, Eddie felt only a small amount of discomfort from the beating he took. Blood remained, metallic tasting, dripping down the back of his throat. He spit out the window a few times. His head throbbed, but as long as he remained unmoving, there was little pain.

Each was quiet, likely thinking as Eddie was, that nothing went according to plan. What was the plan? The grand effort ended badly. Main Street eventually became a route with a number. Eddie couldn't remember the number, though he'd known it his whole life. As they left Barstow, a pale glow on the low horizon announced the sunrise, the next day. Eddie had seen the sunrise many times over the years. He'd always questioned its promises. This was different. Everything had changed, and it was with certainty that he felt he'd seen the last of these false promises. Nothing mattered anymore. Death was too near.

Chapter Five

Morning passed in the car. For some time, Eddie slept. He awoke to Mr. McCoy and Mr. Green talking, nothing heated, just mundane chatter, going nowhere. The desert brightness hammered powerfully as did the wind through the windows. Eddie grimaced when he moved, tried shutting himself off again, seeing only a vivid red within closed eyes. For as long he focused only on the present moment, there was a strange comfort in the distance gained, the hundreds of miles of nothing. He wished he could wash his face, wondered how long it would be before he had soap and a sink. He wondered how long it would be before he saw a bed again. Would it never come?

"Harley Earl. The Y-job."

"Ford put that wrap around windshield on his Thunderbird last year. You see that?"

"I saw it."

Pauses lingered between responses. Was Mary Rose sleeping? Why did they care so much about these stupid designs? What did it matter? Eddie felt so tired he couldn't stand it. Earlier, having gained a considerable distance from Barstow, Mr. Green stopped at a roadside joint, and along with sandwiches and beer, purchased ice for Eddie's face. Mr. Green had gone in alone. What happened once the bank opened? Were there suspicions of Eddie? Had anyone connected it to the two strangers from Los Angeles? Had photographs been published for the mid-day newspapers? With so many unknowns, no one could afford to be spotted except Mr. Green. It was a kind gesture, sympathetic, but what did it really mean?

"Even the Plymouths now come with tailfins."

"Flashy."

"Earl said he was inspired by the P-38, a twin-fuselage fighter plane from the war."

"Drivers think they're flying."

What would Connie and Lou say to their boys? Eddie wondered, and then he wondered if he really cared. Shawn and Paul never took much interest in him, didn't seem to respect him, and probably thought he was odd. Despite a lifetime of tedious routine, Eddie marveled at how much he longed to be at his desk, the same desk he hated. Where had these feelings come from? What good were they? He wished all this was behind him. He wished it could just be a bad dream, a warning from Heaven to stay in line.

"How'd that LeSabre do, the one with heated seats and moisture sensors to raise the top when it starts to rain?"

"Rockefeller probably bought two, the two that sold."

"Uh-huh … See the Lincoln Futura?"

"A picture."

"People don't want to get out of their cars today. They drive to work. At night they're racing in the streets. They go to drive-in restaurants. They watch movies in their hot rods. So different from when I had my garage."

Every mile farther from the Security Pacific tore into Eddie's nerves. How did Mr. Teesdale react to the blood and vomit? Did he immediately race to the safe? Was he disappointed in Eddie? If so, why hadn't he been nicer during the seventeen years Eddie was so loyal?

Were neighbors walking by his house, pointing, commenting, and shaking their heads? What about inside? What was going on? Were his mother and father hovering, walking in the footsteps of memories, unable to speak of their profound heartbreak? How could they have raised such a colossal idiot?

Perhaps they had no idea, Eddie considered. What powers of observation did the after-life provide? Was there a God? Maybe there was no God. Maybe God moved. Maybe he relocated to some other, less costly, universe.

"We're not driving all the way to Tucson, are we?" Mary Rose asked, after what seemed hours of silence.

"The important thing," Mr. McCoy answered, "is for us not to be seen, not even by a pimply clerk in a rat-hole town. We'll take our time, tune in to the radio when we find a frequency, and decide how to proceed based on what news we get. At night, we'll pull off-road, hide where no one can see."

Mr. McCoy disclosed this without a word from Mr. Green. Eddie figured there must have been a discussion while he slept, or a previously agreed upon contingency plan. What would they do with him? he wondered. Obviously, they had no intention of giving Eddie money.

In darkness, under stars, some distance off-road, his life would come to an end. It had to. It was the sensible thing for them to do, Eddie felt. Had it been the plan all along? What from the original plan remained? He believed Mary Rose and Mr. McCoy intended to stay for an undetermined amount of time in Barstow after the heist. They wouldn't have planned to leave two automobiles behind. The abrupt departure raised eyebrows; of that, there could be no doubt. They hadn't planned on that.

If the plan had been to kill Eddie or knock him over the head and toss him into Mr. Green's Coupe to be disposed of in the desert, Mary Rose and Mr. McCoy would have been vulnerable to questions surrounding his disappearance. The chances of them welcoming that had to be zero. The original plan had to be that Eddie would stay alive, at least for a while. Eddie would be at the bank right now if more money had been in that safe.

How many conversations were taking place in Barstow about Eddie? How many customers felt validated in believing him to be an oddball, unconventional? He rarely went to church, never joined in the holiday caroling or the parade. What kind of a man doesn't marry and raise children? He was downright loony. They were right, Eddie guessed. They had his number from the start.

"I want to send a letter to Louise Von Sherman," Mary Rose stated.

"Not now," Mr. McCoy replied firmly.

"She should know I'm still not going to be around for a while."

"She'll figure that out."

Somewhat pleadingly, Mary Rose went on. "Gene, I just want to send her a letter."

"Sent letters can be tracked. Don't be stupid."

"I won't put a name or address on the envelope."

"The post office will stamp it with the name of some town. It'll point to where we've been. Use your head for something brainy for once."

Furious, she shook her head, and her lips mashed together. Eddie was pleased to see Mr. McCoy so heartless toward her, felt she deserved it, not for the letter she hoped to send, but for other things. Yet, he loathed her suffering too. What had she ever seen in such a villain as Mr. McCoy?

"You exaggerate how highly she thinks of you anyways," Mr. McCoy added.

"I do not. She wants me to work at one of her stores."

"She has no stores."

"She will. She's got people in New York interested in her designs."

"Big deal. Probably not even true."

"I'd like to work in a store. I like clothes. I'd be good at that. She thinks so too. She told me."

"Forget it. Drop it. No one wants to listen to this dumb talk. You're not sending any letters. That's all there is to it."

Eddie closed his eyes, but couldn't keep them shut. Was there any chance of escape, any chance to remain alive? Jumbled thoughts, questions, seeped down from his head into his heart, creating a feeling of continuous panic. He wanted to leap from his skin, but he was trapped. The sun, lower than before, burned into oblivion as it fell. It spoke to him, told him this was the end, they were going out together, there was nothing he could do.

Mr. Green slowed suddenly, pressuring the brakes, shifting to the side of the road. "Got to fill the tank," he said to the unspoken questions. The air no longer moved, and the temperature seemed to rise. Mr. McCoy dropped his head back onto the seat and took a deep breath.

Eddie imagined Paris. He strolled Technicolor streets, hand in hand with Mary Rose, passing painters dabbing their canvases, florists, and bullfighters. In an apartment high above the city, before a wall of windows that angled upward toward the moon, she removed her sweater. Eddie touched her soft flesh, could smell the freshness of her perfume. He told her he pushed back the morning flight to Cairo so they could sleep late and enjoy a good breakfast. She turned to him. He kissed her, and made love to her.

Outside the Coupe, Mr. Green struggled with the weight of a gas canister pulled from the trunk. He was clearly in bad health. What reasons had he for doing this? Maybe there was a son or daughter.

He and Mr. McCoy seemed unfamiliar with each other. There was no chumminess, no shared experiences referenced. Therefore, Mr. Green might've been known by reputation, which would mean he was a career criminal. Maybe Mr. Green had some making up to do, and wished for a final act that proved some worth as a father. He was a strange figure, more interesting, Eddie felt, than Mr. McCoy. Was he ruthless? Could his weak appearance be a deception?

He certainly had intelligence. No one in Barstow knew Mr. Green. He didn't exist as far as the bank heist was concerned. Suspicions rained on Eddie, Mary Rose, and Mr. McCoy like a storm of Biblical proportions; of that Eddie could be sure, but above Mr. Green were bright blue skies.

His best bet, as Eddie continued to reflect on Mr. Green, would be to knock off his partners and take all the money. Where would he go? What would he do? Eddie sighed, and stopped thinking about Mr. Green. Why did he care anyway? What difference did it make? The brief expanding of his chest hurt. He closed his eyes, seeing the same vivid red, confident only in his fast approaching demise.

***

A coyote yapped loudly. Was it hunting some critter? Had it been bitten by a snake? No one said anything. Eddie tried putting it out of his mind. He couldn't remember if his previous overnight in the desert had been so cold.

They still hadn't killed him. What could be holding them up? Was it Mary Rose? Could she have warned them she'd go to the police, and therefore they'd have to kill her too? Whatever the reason, whatever her feelings for him, Eddie still felt isolated and targeted.

They hadn't rolled far enough from the road for a fire. Mr. McCoy pointed out they lacked proper wood anyway. Sagebrush tended to burn up in a flash. Eddie didn't know where they were, other than that they'd crossed the Arizona state line. Mary Rose had climbed into the back of the Coupe to stretch out and sleep. Mr. McCoy paced, sat in the dirt, and paced some more. Mr. Green smoked. The hours hidden from the world passed slowly.

Stars filling the night sky relieved some of the loneliness Eddie felt. It was beautiful. Without the blinding power of the sun, the view of other worlds was a reminder that the planet belonged somewhere. No one could comprehend such an expanse, and so it became a place of mystery, Eddie reckoned, a mystery whose narrative people believed would play out well in the end. It was like that with stars. Going as far back as ancient times, people put their hopes in them. Imagine, Eddie silently said to no one, how much more bleak the world would be if the night sky were only black. Imagine no tiny lights to guide ships, no constellations to inspire myths. How did they get there? Where did they come from? Who put them there? Such thoughts, a place to rest his wounded faith, steadied his heart.

The end wouldn't be so bad, he felt. It might be the perfect cure for loneliness. His greatest regret would be all that he missed.

He wished for a way to unburden his sister. Somehow, he knew she was awake at this late hour, in bed, worried. Would she ever know of his concern? How shocked she would be to learn of his sympathies for her. Had his distance caused her to believe he didn't care? Eddie did care. He always cared.

One night, years earlier, just after the war, Connie telephoned. It was late. She was sobbing. Eddie hurried over. Lou had gone too far, drank too much. He stood repentantly, not looking at Eddie. His pupils shook like those of a frightened animal. Lou said only one thing, and Eddie never forgot it: "I'm happy at work."

Connie couldn't stop crying. What should've been the end—a temper tantrum that turned violent—was just the beginning. It certainly wasn't all Lou's fault. He had no idea what he got into when he married her. With everyone around her, Connie had an uncontrollable impulse. She wanted to change them. She was a sculptor, picking and prodding, chipping away character traits she didn't like. Traits she did like corresponded with traits she saw in herself. If met with no resistance, she'd mold everyone into an imitation of her. Exacerbating this most cloying of tendencies was the fact that deep down she repressed an immense dissatisfaction with herself. Consequently, the carving up of other people was without end.

Eddie remembered how carefree Lou was when he first started coming to the house. He and Connie were in their teens at the time. Connie was pretty, and Lou was so in love. Their future seemed promising.

Eddie stood from the desert floor, shivered, and limped off to relieve his bladder. His brain hurt from thinking, and his side still hurt from kicks endured the night before. With his back to the others, he looked up at the stars, slowly closed his eyes, and released a long-winded breath.

A simultaneous explosive crack and burst of light startled Eddie enough to lift him in the air. He spun around and saw a pistol in the hand of Mr. Green. The planet went spinning. Eddie's legs trembled beneath him. He couldn't breathe. The shock put a terrible pain in his chest.

Mr. Green stood stooped. His gun arm bent, waving slowly at the dark blue desert. "I don't know if I got him," he rasped.

"What the hell's going on?" Mary Rose yelled from inside the Coupe.

"You scared him," Mr. McCoy said to Mr. Green. "I'm sure he's gone."

"What was it?" Mary Rose demanded to know.

"Snake," Mr. McCoy answered.

Regaining his ability to breathe, Eddie shook with emotion. Tears dampened his eyes. He rubbed at them before they could cascade down his cheeks. "Maybe ..." Unsteady, Eddie stammered. "Maybe we should get back on the road."

"Don't have a cow," Mr. McCoy said.

A stretch of quiet passed. Mary Rose remained in the car. The men stood frozen, looking like toy soldiers in the moonlight, listening, eager to believe that any cause for alarm had slithered away or died.

***

No other words were traded before sunrise with the exception of Eddie asking about their eventual destination.

"Someplace far," Mr. McCoy responded.

Eddie pressed further. "How long before we get there?"

"We'll be there by this time tomorrow."

Returned to their same positions inside the Coupe, the two sacks of cash somewhat camouflaged by groceries, they withstood an increasingly warm wind jostling clothes and hair. The sky had a near nuclear brightness, and Eddie convinced himself this was the final day of his life. They wanted him as far as possible from Barstow before planting him in the ground.

"You like the comic strips, Eddie?" Mr. McCoy asked.

For a long time Eddie didn't respond. What kind of question was that? Why was he asking? Mr. McCoy repeated the question, louder the second time. Had Mary Rose said something about his radio programs? Were they mocking him?

"Sure. I don't know," Eddie answered elusively, wishing he'd back off.

"Boob McNutt. You read that one?"

Keeping his focus on the barren landscape and hot blue sky, Eddie said nothing. He imagined wrestling Mr. Green's gun away and turning the money in, making up a story about being forced to comply with the demands of these deranged men.

"You know, Eddie, Boob McNutt? He has that Siberian Cheesehound, goes everywhere with him. You a fan?"

"Gene ..." Mary Rose said, slightly turning to the back. She spoke with a reprimanding tone.

"Barney Baxter and his friend Gopher Gus. You like them? What's the matter? You not talking to me?"

"Gene ..."

"Count Screwloose of Tooloose?"

Mary Rose pivoted and locked eyes on Mr. McCoy, insisting, "That's enough."

"Oh, yeah? Who are you to say what I can and can't say? I'm just making conversation."

Thankfully, Mr. McCoy let it go. An hour or more must've passed while no one said a word. Eddie felt their elevation rising, and before long, many miles of southwestern terrain held their spellbound gaze. They'd climbed high up on a hill to an abandoned mining town. As they entered, an eerie stillness met them.

The backs of some buildings had crumbled away. They saw no people. A red camel stood atop a coffee shop. On another corner was an old hotel. Was this their destination? Eddie knew questions wouldn't be answered, so he kept them to himself. A skeletal Hispano-Suiza, probably from the late 1920s, sat sinking in the earth. It looked like the royal dead among a graveyard of rusted metal and wood.

Mr. Green swerved the Coupe around, landing before a General Store. A man was on a bench, the first person they spotted, his attention fallen somewhere deep within. Heat swelling as they idled, Mr. Green hesitated before shutting off the engine. As if reading his mind, Mr. McCoy said, "That bub's not paying attention to anything."

Mr. Green nodded, shut down the Coupe, and pulled the key. He opened the door, squinting. After snatching cigarettes from a breast pocket, he lit one. Birds disturbed the air, lightly tapping on the extreme silence.

Eddie missed his toast and banana, his little table in the kitchen. Somehow, it seemed like someone was still living that life. Everything had changed so fast. He told himself—and it must've been the hundredth time—to calm down. To work himself into a panic would do him no good.

He breathed deeply, audibly, a lungful of hot dry air in, a lungful of hot dry air out, as they all waited for Mr. Green.

They were anxious for news about the heist. The radio picked up a short-lived frequency earlier but they only heard honky-tonk songs. As Eddie looked out the window, face pressed against the sunshine, he saw a cat skip by, dirty on one side. It ran off, frightened by Mr. Green's exit from the General Store. Though everything was less defined without his glasses, Eddie could still see, and his eyes followed the cat as it met with another. They looked comfortable together, had obviously been lurking around the town as a pair, and as he watched, Eddie considered the basic need for companionship among all creatures. He wondered about his affection for Mary Rose. Was it nothing more than an attempt to satisfy a basic need? Who really was she anyway?

A sack of groceries bulged from Mr. Green's stick-like figure. "No newspapers," he said upon returning. "They get a stack from Phoenix most afternoons, but yesterday's are gone."

Frustrated, Eddie sighed. After so much distance, the interminable blindness to any hounds on their trail was unnerving. Eddie could feel them in the thickening air, monsters born from guilt ready to pounce, but nowhere to be seen.

"Look," Mr. McCoy said, pointing outward from beside Eddie. He'd spotted a rolled up newspaper protruding from a trashcan. "Might not be recent enough but it's worth a shot."

Mr. Green left the groceries and went for the newspaper. He scanned the ramshackle town, saw no one watching, pulled the newspaper from the trash, spread it open, combed the columns, and then his face slowed. Had he found something? Were suspects named? Finally, with the newspaper wedged under his arm, and bad news hanging on his tongue, he walked back to the car.

Eddie had to get out. He was boiling. Eyes were on fire from the brightness. He couldn't go anywhere though. Mr. McCoy would catch him, and even if he could get away, where would he go? Desert was everywhere. If lucky enough to reach authorities, what would he say?

"There's an article about the heist." Mr. Green rasped, handing the folded newspaper to Mr. McCoy. "Not much. Mentions Eddie's name but nobody else."

Mr. McCoy read the article aloud. Each word fell like a hammer on a nail. What about the mess on the carpet, blood and vomit? How could anyone possibly conclude Eddie was alone?

"Let's get out of here," Mr. McCoy said, setting the newspaper aside. "Doesn't really give us much."

"Strange they didn't mention the amount of money." As Eddie said this, he gently climbed aboard a line of thinking that could put a little time in his pocket. The article triggered a need for him to defend himself. He would find this time with a lie. It rushed to him, and he let it spill from his lips as it came to him. "Just seems odd, that's all. Mr. Teesdale always told me there was never less than seventy-five thousand dollars in the safe. 'There's seventy-five thousand dollars in the safe, always.' That's what he'd say. He was consistent, told me that for years. Seventy-five thousand. So, why was there less? I don't know if I have a point to make, I'm just saying there's a woman, Ms.—I can't remember her first name—Oh, yes, Alice. Alice Meyer. She lives in a little house. I know where it is. I know the address. Ms. Meyer would come in and make sizable cash withdrawals. Mr. Teesdale insisted he'd deal with Ms. Meyer personally. What's interesting— looking back now—is that every time Ms. Meyer would come in, Mr. Teesdale would go to the safe. Every time. I did ask Mr. Teesdale if he knew where she sends all that cash, and he said she keeps it in a closet. When I asked for her reasons he said she worries the bank will go out of business. We never could tell how much money he'd give her, just that it was a lot. Her account was never notated in the ledgers. Mr. Teesdale insisted it was unnecessary. You can imagine the rumors passed between me and the other employees at the bank. I always thought it was an affair but Sue and Lynette thought it was something more nefarious."

Mr. McCoy said, "That's awful fancy. Sounds crazy."

"Fine," Eddie replied easily. "I'm not the kind of person who makes up stories. I have little imagination. I'm just telling you—"

"I still don't get it. Why's it strange the newspapers didn't mention the money?"

"If they said I stole forty-eight thousand dollars then Security Pacific headquarters might wonder why the safe was carrying less than seventy-five thousand. Maybe Mr. Teesdale didn't want that information made public. I don't know. Look, I don't care if you believe me or not. What difference does it make? Making up stories isn't going to do me, or anybody, any good. What would be the point of me doing so? Ms. Meyer's house is all the way back in Barstow anyway. We would be nuts to go back there."

***

Though it was evening, Eddie thought back to the breakfast he had with Mary Rose at The Continental. Bacon and eggs, coffee, cinnamon toast and pancakes; it hardly seemed real. By day's end, they all must've been thinking, as Eddie was, about food and a soft bed with cool clean sheets.

Most of the day passed silently. Mr. McCoy seemed agitated a lot of the time. Eddie wondered if it was about Ms. Meyer in Barstow. Was he thinking about getting his hands on that cash? Would he keep Eddie alive until he got the address out of him? Eddie had no answers. He could only hope Mr. McCoy might be foolish enough and greedy enough to think about returning to Barstow.

He imagined sitting in the house he lived in his whole life, watching—as it was again Friday—Bob Cummings and *Dragnet*. How much easier everything would've been had he never left that simple world.

Yet his heart still ached for Mary Rose. She accompanied his constant thoughts, and he caught himself casting adoring glances even when turned away. She had defended him against Mr. McCoy's viciousness. She had to have feelings for him. She was decent. The train carrying her just went off course somewhere. Eddie could see how it happened to people.

Earlier, they saw a sign that read: four hundred miles to Los Angeles. Eddie imagined Los Angeles as a wonderful place, and hated passing the new road. Would he ever see Hollywood? What was Cary Grant doing tonight? he wondered. Probably sipping champagne, surrounded by other film stars, wallowing in the devoted swoon of a woman who looked almost as great as Mary Rose.

"We have enough!"

From a distance, Eddie turned to the sound of Mary Rose shouting. She got out of the Coupe and made a dramatic slam of the car door behind her. Mr. McCoy chased her. They quieted, but anger was visible in animated gestures and hushed strained voices. Eddie wondered if their fighting had something to do with him. What could it be? How far would it go?

Mr. Green sat on a large rock, also distant from them, coughing and smoking, incurious. What had gone wrong in his life? What bad road led him here? The fight went on for a while and Mr. Green offered it not so much as a glance.

For the first time Eddie considered that maybe he was smarter than his cohorts. Having turned off the southbound road with enough daylight for Mr. Green to dodge dry sunken paths, they'd traveled a good distance. After bumping around for fifteen minutes or so, Eddie got nervous. Was this it? But when stars came out and night fell and two hours went by with Mr. McCoy and Mr. Green seemingly lost in thoughts far removed from Eddie, he came to believe he'd survive another night. Was it thanks to Ms. Meyer, an old woman who didn't even exist?

Mr. McCoy, alone, walked back to Mr. Green's automobile. He got inside, disappearing in the darkness. Eddie guessed he was still upset. Unlike the night before, moonlight painted no glistening scribbles on the Coupe. Dust and dirt exhausted her pride.

Should he go to Mary Rose? She stood facing none of them. She looked only a little like the woman Eddie first saw at the Security Pacific. She held herself differently, defensively. The stars seemed sad above her.

To his surprise, Eddie suddenly felt no comfort in the stars. Where he felt closeness before, he now felt the unfathomable distance. The stars seemed created only to clarify his insignificance in the world. He felt like nothing, and wondered if he went over and stole a kiss from Mary Rose, would she even feel it? Would she even look up, or would it be like he wasn't even there?

Hours later, seated on the ground, and propped against a rock, Eddie, who had been sleeping for at least an hour, awakened to a sound. A deep royal blue filled the sky and it fell into the colors of a peach at the horizon. Eddie stood, slightly alarmed, and dusted his slacks. Mr. Green remained sleeping. Mary Rose and Mr. McCoy were unseen.

Eddie heard the sound a second time, and could now with certainty decipher it as Mary Rose's voice. While still parked, engine off, exactly where it had been for many hours, the Coupe shook. The tires were unmoving, firmly planted, but the body plunged and bucked. The sound came again, a moan.

Mary Rose's moans cried from the car, soon calling out with the rhythm of a slow train. Not the high-pitched sounds of her speaking voice, these deep-throated wails came from a repeated filling up and releasing of all the air in her lungs.

Realizing what was happening, the intensity of it quickening, Eddie's throat went dry. He stood paralyzed. Had Mr. McCoy forced himself upon her? Was she in pain, or was he listening to screams of pleasure?

Seating himself on the rock, he put his head in his hands. The world was spinning, and he thought he might be sick. Gradually, the voice diminished to mutterings, and then nothing. Eddie looked up to the sound of a car door opening. Mr. McCoy stumbled from within the Coupe, and swaggered off into the still dark desert, his open belt buckle rattling as he went. Mary Rose's head lifted from the backseat. She turned to where Eddie sat. A second later, she turned away.

Eddie felt like he'd entered a room behind the little room he'd always lived in. The lies he told himself had felt so true in his heart that now nothing made sense. Dizzy, feeling his body grossly enlarged, he imagined scrambling back to where he was before, but no longer fit. He pressed his eyes shut. How could she? What possessed her? She must hate me, he thought, and she couldn't care less that he knew it.

Silence was thick in the air, barely allowing for Mr. McCoy's distant footsteps. Something got Eddie to his feet, and he took a bold step. Mr. Green hadn't moved. With his back to Eddie, roughly thirty feet away, Mr. McCoy relieved his bladder. Listening to the trickle of urine, Eddie took another step in the direction of the Coupe.

He didn't give it much thought, just hustled with soft footfalls to the automobile, and opened the driver's side door. When they first parked, in the early hours of the previous evening, they forgot to check for a radio signal. Hours later, Mr. McCoy asked for the keys, but his attempt to pull some news out of the air came to nothing. Eddie counted on the wild chance the keys were left in the ignition.

He saw them dangling under the steering wheel. He questioned his eyesight. It was too easy, he thought. Breathless, he glanced into the backseat. Eyes shut, Mary Rose looked oblivious. Spinning again to the front, Eddie brought the engine to life. He punched the accelerator with his right foot, and shut the door. Looking up, Mary Rose cried, "Eddie! What're you doing?" The Coupe lurched, slipping a little on dry earth.

Like a feral dog, Mr. McCoy's voice barked outrage in the background, cries Eddie couldn't make out. Eddie didn't bother with the rearview though, as it was hard to spot ditches and creosote bushes even following the beams of his now blazing headlights.

Her panic firing on all cylinders at this point, Mary Rose continued, "Eddie, stop!"

The Coupe pounded into an embankment, jolting Eddie hard into the wheel. The car then skidded off, kicking up dry dirt before rocketing forward again. Something hammered on the trunk. Eddie spun around and saw Mr. McCoy leap onto Mr. Green's car and claw for something to grasp. After picking up his best speed, Eddie pulled down hard on the wheel, snapping the rear of the vehicle around, and when Eddie next looked, Mr. McCoy was gone.

"They'll kill you, Eddie. This isn't some game. Stop! Eddie!"

As morning light increased, Eddie's navigation improved. He looked back quickly at Mary Rose and saw groceries on the floor, the cash as well.

Beyond the cracked and brittle wasteland, he looked for the road. He put the glow of the eastern sun at his back, knowing they'd turned left after traveling southbound. Grabbed again by some hungry hole in the desert, the car dropped beneath him, and then tossed him side to side.

Regaining control, he stomped on the accelerator, fearing the slow down might allow Mr. McCoy to catch up. He saw no one, however, and could barely make out what he perceived to be a smoothing of the landscape ahead.

"Eddie, if you're not going to stop, at least let me out. I don't know where you're going or what you're doing. Eddie, did I tell you I'm sorry? I'm sorry for what happened. I feel positively awful about it. Stop the car, Eddie."

He swerved onto the road and climbed from zero to sixty in minutes while ignoring an earful of protests from behind. He had no plan, didn't even want to think of a plan. Moving fast was Eddie's only thought, getting away, running from everything that had happened.

"Eddie!" Kicking the seat now, Mary Rose became unhinged. "Stop the car!"

Her hysterical behavior surprised him. Was he still refusing to believe she despised him? She had become an obsession, and he told himself he had to let it go. He had to forget about her. She didn't like him. Nothing would change that.

He put his weight on the brake, brought the Coupe to a painful stop. There was nothing around. The planet seemed empty and the stars began to fade. Eddie let the engine idle, waiting for Mary Rose to go. He heard the back door open, and then he leaned to the backseat with a last minute concern.

As she stood with the car door open, Eddie handed her the two sacks filled with forty-eight thousand dollars. "Good luck," he muttered.

She gripped the cash. "Eddie ..." she said.

"It's okay."

"But I ..."

"Just go."

She shut the door. Eddie shifted into drive and rolled forward, gently picking up speed. She was no good, he told himself. She was selfish, looking for a ride on easy street. He deserved better. He watched her falling behind in his rearview, standing with the money in her hands, her pretty head angled to the pavement, not going anywhere.

Eddie saw her shoulders tremble. She shuddered, and the back of a hand brushed a cheek. She was crying. Eddie stopped, and though they were probably a good thirty yards apart, her face lifted to him.

She was so tempting, Eddie thought, and he wanted her to love him more than anything. His chest pounded and hope swelled as she straightened herself, and then he saw the most astonishing sight he ever could've imagined. She walked toward him. Her steps were timid at first, but gained confidence as she neared. Eddie put the Coupe in reverse and rolled back to her. She got into the passenger seat, and with a rising sun at his side, Eddie gunned the first car he ever had down the open road. She'd made her choice.

Chapter Six

Eddie peeked outside through a motel room's closed curtains. The day hadn't ended yet, but the intensity of light had waned. Eager for Mary Rose's return, and not seeing her, he turned back to the lonely lamp-lit room.

Lordsburg was one hundred and fifty miles east of Tucson. A line of Christmas-colored tinsel draped over Main Street. It was a tiny town, aged, with nothing much to show aside from survival. Everything looked comfortable though, inviting. Just outside of town, sun-beaten and bedraggled, was the Border Motel. It was like something from a movie, Eddie thought, when they first saw it, and thought Mary Rose seemed less sensitive to its tawdriness than he. Was she accustomed to shabby rooms? As he considered it, nothing ever seemed to surprise her.

With Mr. McCoy and Mr. Green gone, Mary Rose had a few ideas about doing things differently, like no more of this sleeping and eating in the car business, and Eddie agreed wholeheartedly.

After she left to pick up a few things, Eddie had tried to rest on the bed, but with stress clawing at him from every direction, his brain wouldn't stop spinning. The money, on the other hand, lit a wild flame in his heart. He was an outlaw, he'd reflected with mixed feelings. Getting up from his failed attempt at rest, he'd spread bills all over the room, the whole forty-eight grand. After covering the bed, the floor, and the dresser, he stood back and imagined Mary Rose's eyes upon seeing such an extraordinary vision when she returned.

Standing with his back to the window now, Eddie thought of his old friend Lowell, the first time in a long while. They'd spent nearly every day together in the early 1930s. They'd talked endlessly of motion pictures, and laughed uproariously at stories made up about their favorite characters' off-screen lives. When The Barstow opened and everyone raved about sound pictures and air conditioning, Eddie and Lowell fondly recalled to each other the nights when Douglas Fairbanks or Lon Chaney came alive on the side of a building, and the town brought chairs, and a violinist played for tips. Something about transforming a brick building into another world beneath a sky crowded with stars put magic in the night in a way that words from lips never could. One day Lowell announced he'd received a letter from a Chicago company offering him a job. He'd talked about the cold he'd have to adjust to, and was gone. They said they'd write but never did. Eddie imagined Lowell must still enjoy talking about movies. He probably eventually got a new friend, a wife too, maybe children. Was he talking about Eddie now, having seen him in the newspapers, and saying he knew this crook throughout his youthful days in Barstow? Unquestionably, many heads were shaking in disbelief.

Not wanting to think about Lowell anymore—it was a lifetime ago—Eddie clicked on a radio. A modern-day song played, and the music was lean and had a swing. Without belting, the voice had a richness that hit the floor and ceiling at the same time. The singer crooned about thunder, a troubled past, and a ribbon of concrete offering promise. The guitar pierced like a hammering of spikes. Eddie mimed picking strings. Rattling his head as he listened, the song became a transfusion, filling him with rebel blood. He raised the volume.

The room brightened suddenly. Mary Rose stood with two bags, a scarf over her head, and a funny look on her face. A lit cigarette dangled from her lips. "My goodness. You've changed," she said, assessing Eddie, the cash-flooded room, and the snap-shuffle of the rock and roll. She kicked the door shut, ending the new brightness.

"What'd you find?" he asked, lowering the radio's volume.

Holding up a bag, she answered, "From the diner I got broasted chicken, peas and potatoes with butter, and an apple pie. I also stopped at a liquor store and got a bottle of whisky." She removed her scarf, set the bags down and joked in response to the cash, "Redecorating?"

"I just thought you'd—I don't know—what's in the other bag?"

"Dye, plus other cosmetics. Starting tomorrow morning I'll have black hair."

Minutes later, they sat on the floor, their backs against the bed, shoveling food in their faces with plastic forks. Eddie liked having her close. She seemed untroubled by the days ahead, but as he couldn't help stealing glances at her soft round forms, he thought of what she had been doing in the back of Mr. Green's Coupe not even a day earlier. He said nothing about it. What good would it do to bring it up? He learned that Mr. Green had once been a safe technician, familiar with combination locks of all sorts. Mr. McCoy's last name was really Green. Eugene was his true first name, and therefore he went by the odd name of Gene Green. Mary Rose said she didn't know the safe technician's real name. Eddie sipped whiskey from their only glass, while Mary Rose drank straight from the bottle.

"What's your real name?" Eddie asked, his words falling off a whiskey-soaked tongue.

"My first name is Mary. My last name is Rose," she smiled.

"See any s'newspapers?"

With a giggle, Mary Rose mocked his slurring, "Snooze papers?"

"Newspapers. What'd I say?" Turning red, Eddie mumbled, "Good whiskey."

Mary Rose raised the bottle and announced, "No more snooze papers. They just tell you what you don't want to hear." She knocked back a gulp, put a cheerful face to him, and then refilled his glass. "Eddie," she said, "this motel looks like shit."

His eyebrows hit the ceiling. He was unaccustomed to such language from a woman. She suddenly seemed the type who lured trouble her way. Why hadn't he seen it before? She was Gloria Grahame. Could she be different with an assistant bank manager? "You're just now noticing?"

"Someone should paint blue skies and green pastures on these walls."

In his imagination, Eddie pictured the unusual idea and added a touch of his own. "And a doggie."

"That's right. A doggie. Maybe some rabbits. Make it look like you're outside when you're really inside. Fluffy white clouds. Why doesn't anybody do that?"

"People like walls. Makes them feel secure, I guess."

Her eyes fluttered with exhaustion. "I can't eat anymore," she muttered.

"It was delicious. What're we gonna do with the rest of the apples pie?"

Lit up with laughter again, she said, "Wait. Did you say apple spy?"

Eddie laughed as her giggling grew to where she could hardly form words. Eventually she caught her breath, and then calmed down, and said, "What do you suppose happened to the two Mr. Greens?"

Eddie thought for a second before smiling, and then he replied, "I don't give a shit."

"They probably got a good suntan today," she surmised.

"See, we did them a favor."

"I'm going to have another bite of this pie just to spite their starving stomachs. Fools. Let them rot in hell."

"I'm gonna have another bite too," Eddie gushed.

"Except for this dump, we're living like kings, Eddie."

"I don't know how we got here. It's strange, but I feel like I'm just sort of along for the ride, like I have no say in the matter. What're we doing? How'd we get here? Where are we going? Is there any way we can survive this?"

"Don't think so much. Don't ask so many questions. Eat some more apple spy."

The night ended with them sharing the bed, fully clothed, the whiskey bottle emptied, sleeping as if they'd been awake for a year.

***

Once, when Eddie was little, he fell out of a moving car. The incident prompted an argument between his mother and father about whether or not he was dumb. Eddie had been in the back seat. A neighbor had taken him and his mother for a drive and as they slowed, Eddie wanted out. After opening the door, he clumsily tripped. The neighbor slammed on the brakes, and Eddie's mother started shouting. The car looked like a Model T, but as Eddie always remembered, it seemed nicer than a Model T. It was one of a growing number of automobiles in Barstow at the time. In the passenger seat while Mary Rose drove, thinking back on the forty-three-year-old incident, Eddie wondered if he'd ever forget his angry father's efforts to have his son's brain tested for missing pieces.

"We need a map," Mary Rose insisted.

"Are you good with maps?"

"I've never used one."

She didn't look like Jane Russell, as he thought she might. She looked like a raven-haired Marilyn Monroe. Her speech was slightly different. She now had a snappy tone, whereas previously she spoke with the sound of wide-eyed innocence. Hidden layers emerged, a haunted look masked by toughness, and fast grabs at cigarettes spoke of old wounds or new insecurities, Eddie couldn't tell. He knew only that the woman he first met was a small piece of someone far more complicated. "We should see if we can get some news," Eddie suggested. "It would be helpful, like if it says the Barstow bank robber was seen on the southern border we could head north to Canada."

"Canada's not north."

"What do you mean Canada's not north? Of course it is."

"It is?"

"Where do you think it is?"

"Is it east?"

"It's north. I just told you. How old are you?"

"Don't condescend to me."

Surprised by her feistiness, not meaning to be rude, Eddie politely clarified, "I'm not. I just assumed most Americans knew where Canada was."

"Well, when you see a newsstand let me know," she said, sarcastically referring to the empty desert.

"You know, I've been thinking," Eddie began after a moment. "Maybe if we anonymously return the money, send it back in a package, they'll let us go."

"Are you nuts?"

"We don't even know where we're going. We don't have a plan."

"Eddie, you broke the law. If they let you go, then every future bank robber who thinks he's about to get caught will send the money back and get a lawyer to argue, 'Well, you let Eddie Howard go, so you have no grounds to arrest my client.' You can't rob a bank, Eddie. It's the law."

"I didn't rob a bank."

"Yes, you did."

"I tried to stop it."

"I was shocked when you agreed to be involved. It was so stupid."

"I'm just saying maybe they won't pursue us so aggressively."

"You never should have done it in the first place."

For a while, sitting stunned and a little annoyed, Eddie said nothing. Among the number of things he could've said, none were anything less than an attack, and she was so beautiful. In addition to that, she was his only friend. "You know, I think it would be best if we focus on where we go from here."

"I say we go to New York City."

"Why?"

"I've always wanted to go to New York City. Have you ever been?"

"No, I've never been anywhere. Have you been to New York City?"

"No, that's what I'm saying, I've always wanted to go. Plus, they have so many people, we'll blend in."

"You have a driver's license, right?"

"Of course I do."

"Well, you can't just get another one with a new name."

"Condescending again, Eddie. I know that. I know you can't just turn in your old driver's license and say, 'I want a new one with a different name.' But my name is Mary Rose and yours is Eddie Howard. Simple names. There must be a million people with the same names as us."

"Linked to bank robbery?"

"I don't know."

"Sometimes you say things that are smart and sometimes ... I don't know, I wonder."

"Fuck off."

"And the language! I'm shocked. It's not ladylike."

"No, it's not. I agree."

"I don't get you."

"Who says you have to?"

Frustrated, Eddie mashed his lips together, shook his head, and then closed the ornery conversation by saying, "Boy, you're really something when you get going."

The New Mexico skies and the Texas skies were unbelievably huge. As Eddie thought it through, he decided the many clouds hovering against the blue and then shrinking in the distance stretched the sky farther than in Barstow, where such clouds weren't as common. The size of each individual cloud was well defined. These were thick clouds, and each had a pale greenish-gray belly outlined with blinding hot white. The same white fire framed each tuft of desert growth, and put a clear definition to the midday's short shadows. Nothing escaped the up-close scrutiny of the sun.

They traveled through El Paso, which was the largest city Eddie had ever seen. He couldn't get over its stateliness, the grand hotels. It was a bustling western metropolis. Why had he not explored the world more? He'd seen nothing outside of Barstow. Movies had always ignited his imagination and curiosity about big cities and far away lands, yet he never ventured outside his little town, never deviated from his familiar routines. Before leaving El Paso—they had been tempted to stay—Mary Rose bought a map. The old man who sold it to her outlined the best route for crossing the state.

After a long silence, Mary Rose asked, "Are you and I okay?"

"What do you mean?"

She sounded strangely vulnerable as she explained, "You haven't been saying anything. You were talkative and now you're not. I just thought—I was wondering if you were upset with me. I can be moody."

"I was just thinking how different everything is. I wasn't trying to shut you out. Sometimes I have conversations in my head with myself. They go on until one side bores the other side to tears."

"That must not take long."

Eddie said nothing, unsure how to respond. Confusing him further, she punched him and said, "I'm teasing you, stupid. Lighten up."

***

Much later in the day, a million violet clouds burned orange at their frayed edges. The sunset reached in through the rear passenger window, and the vision of it gave Eddie the feeling of having put all of life's wounds in the past. Land and sky were expansive, far-reaching. The highway stretched railroad straight.

Mary Rose offered a few details about her background but not many. Her father was a politician, not on a national level, and only for a few years, and then he became an advisor and a fundraiser and something else before serving on various state boards in Kansas. While relaying tidbits from her youth, her voice fluctuated between conceit and reticence. A few times she started to say something and stopped. Of her mother, she said nothing at all. "I don't really talk to them anymore," she stated as punctuation to the topic. When Eddie asked why, she said, "People do the wrong thing sometimes, but when you're a parent it's your job to try to make it right."

She seemed so different from the woman Eddie met a couple of months earlier. He tried offering comfort, as she appeared to be painting a sad picture of her past, but his words matched her lack of specificity, and as such, provided a poor remedy to her troubles.

Judging from signs, it looked as if they'd arrive in Marfa by nightfall. Eddie had never heard of Marfa, but the old man who sold Mary Rose the map said it had a nice hotel and they should have no trouble getting there by early evening.

Fascinated by the map, Eddie said, "We're so close to Mexico. I wonder if it doesn't make sense to go down there and find a place for a while."

"I don't want to," Mary Rose said.

"Why not?"

"We don't have a Mexican map. We could cross the border and drive until we run out of gas, and we don't speak the language. Our money is American. We'd have to get it turned into Mexican money, and what if there's no place to do that right across the border?"

"We could inquire about it in Marfa."

"We wouldn't be able to drink the water."

"We wouldn't be able to drink the water?"

"You can't drink it as an American."

"You're not allowed?"

"Mexican water makes Americans sick."

"That's crazy. I've never heard that."

"It's true."

"Is the air un-breathable if you're American?"

"Eddie, it's true."

"That's the most outrageous thing I've ever heard. If you buy Mexican jelly beans, will the purple ones give you leprosy?"

"Look, maybe it's a myth, but I've heard it my whole life."

"Well, with age comes a little wisdom."

"Is that why your face is beat up and you're running from the law?"

Struggling for a response, Eddie shook his head. Where had these insults come from, the excessive shifts in attitude? Was this really the same person from Halloween? She seemed so disinterested in him, so dismissive, even combative.

The map led them to the corner of Highland Street and Texas Street. A Spanish Colonial structure towered majestically in a town with little else to see. Excited by the old world luxury and foreign charm of the place, Eddie thought back to Wallace Beery as Pancho Villa. What history had this hotel seen? Mary Rose went in alone to check availability, tell them her "father" was parking the car. They still had no idea if photographs of him had been published with news articles, but Eddie felt certain no recent photographs of him existed. He couldn't remember the last time someone took his picture.

When he finally entered, his eyes combed warm low lights, a tiled floor, exposed wood ceiling beams, a wrought iron chandelier. He'd never seen anything like it.

Upon spotting him, Mary Rose quickly said, "All set, father. We're just upstairs."

Prior to following her, a framed black and white photograph caught Eddie's eye. He stopped. Within the photograph, seated on patio chairs, amid the same architecture as the hotel, were Elizabeth Taylor and a laughing Rock Hudson. "What's this?" he asked the concierge.

"That's Rock Hudson and Elizabeth Taylor. They were here a year ago shooting a motion picture."

"Did they stay here at the hotel?"

"Yes."

"Right here?"

"Yes."

Eddie stood with big eyes, his jaw hung open. Mary Rose nestled an impatient hand under his arm, which he ignored. He whirled to the concierge again, pleading for details. "What picture? What were they like? Were they nice?"

"*Giant*. It's just been released, and I understand it's getting a lot of attention. They were very cordial. Signed autographs. Seemed to be good people."

"That's extraordinary."

Pulling his arm now, Mary Rose interjected, "We're right upstairs, Dad."

Eddie followed, head shaking in disbelief, as they climbed from the lobby to the mezzanine. The room was beautiful and clean. On one side, French doors opened to a private walled patio with a table, chairs, and a fireplace. Mary Rose ordered dinner. A short while later, a man arrived with fried chicken, potato salad, pickles, a beer, a coke, and a slice of cheesecake to share. They ignited a fire and ate while staring into the crackling blaze. The desert night was cool. They didn't say much. Eddie mentioned Rock Hudson a number of times. She reminded him of their situation in an effort to bring him back to reality, and he replied, "This is reality. Rock Hudson was really here. And also, didn't you tell me to stop worrying, stop asking questions about what we're doing, where we're going?"

When they quieted again, Eddie considered that maybe he was desperately trying to return to who he was before. Maybe his fascination with the hotel's esteemed guests was not a good thing. Thinking through his newer feelings, and the changes going on inside him, he began thinking of how she had changed so remarkably. He considered how different she was from before, and wondered again if maybe she had pretended to be someone she wasn't in order to lure him into the heist.

If true, was this not worth it? If even for this one night, staying where Rock Hudson and Elizabeth Taylor stayed months earlier, sitting under the stars on a private patio with a wood fire burning, and a beautiful but potentially deceitful woman, was it not worth going to jail should fate demand such a cost?

***

The next morning, Eddie figured with the heist money they could stay at the hotel for forty-two months. This would leave ten thousand dollars for food to cover the duration. They could hide, live the same bliss every day for twelve hundred and sixty days, see very few people, and even perhaps bribe the concierge on the chance they seemed suspicious. While he was considering the possibility, Mary Rose said, "Let's go, Eddie. No one is going to help us hide from the police."

Walking to the Coupe, her sudden matter-of-factness bringing him back to a full awareness of their circumstances, Eddie saw a phone booth. Stopping, he said, "I'm going to make a fast telephone call."

"Are you sure that's smart? Who're you calling?"

"I'm sure it's not smart," he replied flippantly. "It'll just take a second." He wanted to set things straight with his sister, lessen her concerns. She likely had ideas about him that caused more alarm than necessary. Though life took a wild turn, he wasn't as miserable as he'd been, and he felt compelled to help her see that. Should he mention Lou? Should he point out how her life was far from perfect too? He wasn't sure if he'd ever see her again. Why not get it all out?

He called collect and charges were accepted. Connie's voice, though tight, shook. He heard deep breaths, a rise of emotion, and as he had so many times throughout their adult lives, he wondered how this woman could also be the baby sister he knew three and a half decades earlier.

"Eddie, your picture is everywhere, television, newspapers, they talk about you on the radio. It's all anyone's been talking about. I walk into noisy rooms and everyone turns quiet because they know you're my brother. The police have questioned us more than once. Where are you? What're you doing? You've created a nightmare. People are furious. Are you all right? Are you coming home? You need to get home."

Stunned, feeling reality slithering toward him like an enemy, he looked to the people of Marfa going about their morning. How stupid, he realized, for him to have stepped into the public square. In his imagination he heard sirens racing toward him, could see the triumph among officers, congratulations for apprehending the bad man.

"They say you robbed a bank."

"Don't listen to that. It's not … Connie, I called …"

"Is it true? I have to know if it's true, Eddie."

"No. Yes. I don't know. You're not going to understand."

"It's that woman."

Eddie took a breath. His eyes flared at a cluster of suited men walking toward him with briefcases.

"I told you. I told you, Eddie …"

"Stop saying that. Don't say that. Don't say, 'I told you.'"

"You're a fugitive."

The word sank in. He said nothing for a moment. What had he done? How much trouble had he gotten himself into?

"Eddie, you need to turn yourself in."

With a long breath, he focused himself. "Okay, look, Connie, I called to say good-bye."

She didn't respond. He let the silence stretch between them. He kissed her once. They were children. The family had taken the car out to Calico one Sunday. The day was excruciatingly hot, and they just wanted to feel the rushing air on their faces. Behind a barn, Eddie roamed, and when his little sister followed, he quickly kissed her, undoubtedly inspired by some film star he'd wished to be like. "Connie, are you there?"

"You're not coming back?"

"Listen, I should tell you something else. I never liked Lou. I should've told you before. I should've been honest …"

"What? Eddie, are you out of your mind? Why …"

"Connie, I also want to say … just listen to me … I wish I'd been different. It was stupid of me, unfair, to hold you accountable for Lou, and maybe he wasn't such a bad guy. He's probably a good guy, and I didn't give him a chance. I just didn't understand. People can do bad things and it doesn't necessarily mean they're bad. He's got his disappointments, I'm sure. I've never been good with people. I think I had these ideas about how things were supposed to be. I don't know. I just … it was never you, Connie. You've done a fine job as a person."

"Eddie …"

"No, that's it. I got to go."

"You're like mom."

"What?"

"You want everything perfect."

"I don't know."

"Why did you do this?"

"Who knows? It was something I had to do, I guess. I thought it would make me feel alive."

"That's ridiculous. Did it? Did it make you feel alive? I don't even know what that means. What does that mean? Did committing a crime make you feel good? That's crazy."

"I know."

"Then why did you do it?"

"Remember how terrified mom always was? Remember how she worried about everything? She worried about her worrying, and because of that, she did very little with her life. She mostly just let Dad yell at her. She was like a mouse living behind a wall … I don't want to be like that. I'm not a fucking mouse."

"You think she should have robbed a bank? You think she should've used curse words?"

"I have to go."

"What do I tell people?"

Irritated, Eddie snapped, "Tell them I have zero interest in potluck. Tell them parades have never been fun. I don't know. Tell them I found them all terribly uninteresting."

"Including me?"

"Tell them the truth, Connie. Tell them I'm selfish. Tell them I'm the only person I've ever really been interested in."

"Eddie ..."

Before hanging up, he pinched his eyes closed. She knew him better than anyone, had seen him at his worst, and had never abandoned him. "Good-bye, Connie."

Minutes later, he and Mary Rose jumped on the open road and shot out of Marfa.

Chapter Seven

Eddie debated whether he should reveal to Mary Rose what his sister said about his picture being everywhere. Connie had to guess at Mary Rose's involvement and, therefore, the reporting must not have mentioned her, at least not yet. Potentially, Mary Rose could walk away, take the money and go, but Eddie didn't want her to go. He admitted to his sister that he was selfish. Now he was asking himself to what degree. If caught fleeing with Eddie, her life could be destroyed. Exposed as an accomplice, she'd go to jail, whereas right now there seemed to be nothing anyone had on her. Surely there were unknowns. It's possible law enforcement was looking into the potential involvement of the blond woman who had been staying at the Town & Country, but right now she seemed to be in the clear.

She'd hate him if she knew he was putting her in danger, but were her current feelings anything like love? What were Mary Rose's feelings? Did she have any? Eddie reminded himself of the secrets she had kept from him. All his life he'd known couples that stayed together for decades; was there not a certain amount of selfishness, fear of being alone, fear of losing someone, which triggered manipulations, even lies? Was his silence really so bad, so uncommon?

For now, instead of including her in on what he knew, he directed the conversation toward escape. They went over multiple options, settling on a few ideas. Each thought a change of identity would push the past further behind them, though they were unsure how to go about doing such a thing. Neither had reservations about becoming someone new. In fact, Eddie liked the idea. The problem was simply where to turn for believable documentation. Florida became their best gamble they felt. The drive would provide time to determine the aggressiveness of any pursuit. In addition, they were both attracted to the possibility of running to Cuba should it become necessary to leave the country. Cuba sounded exotic and exciting; a sensible place to take forty-eight grand in cash, and it was only an hour's flight off the Florida coast.

With that agreed to, at least for the time being, Eddie returned to the question of her feelings about him, and the manipulations he'd obviously suffered. He wondered aloud, "What about that scarf you said you lost, the one that belonged to your mother? If you'd continued on to Los Angeles, rather than having returned for your scarf, I never would've been involved in the heist."

"What are you asking me?"

"Why did you return to Barstow for your mother's scarf?"

"Why are you asking about that?"

"Well, didn't you become my friend so I could help you and Gene rob the bank?"

"No," she replied, before quickly changing her mind. "Yes. It's not easy to explain. The idea of getting you involved came about gradually."

"So, had you remembered the scarf when you first left, I wouldn't be here right now. I'd be at work."

"Maybe. I don't know. Gene and I were on the phone. We had a fight. It was about you. I didn't want you involved. I got angry and left, and then I realized I forgot my scarf. Would Gene have convinced me to go back if I hadn't forgotten it? I don't know. He can be very persuasive, as you know."

Visibly deflated, perhaps now recognizing the impact her transforming identities have had on Eddie, she asked, "Are you disappointed in me?"

"I'm not disappointed," Eddie quickly answered before confessing, "I just don't understand how someone as nice as you would want to be with a man like Gene."

For some time, Mary Rose talked about the man she had been with, and Eddie listened. At first, she struggled to explain the connection between the two of them. From her words, Eddie gathered that Gene's hold on her was born out of sympathy. "When he was fourteen, his father told him to leave. Just like that. 'Get out.' Can you imagine? The family had no money, no work. He'd become a burden. He hopped freight trains, spent six years crossing the country, back and forth, feeding on scraps, living like a stray dog. Railroad cops gave him a hard time, constantly chasing him away. Once he was clubbed over the head and ran over snow-covered farmlands, holding onto his gushing wound, spilling blood all over the snow. Eventually, in some small town, I can't remember where, he picked up skills as a mechanic. Wandering through the southwest, he spread the word he could fix a tractor or truck, anything mechanical. He would take a day's work, an hour's work, go anywhere there might be a job. He finally got something in Elko. That's in Nevada. That worked out for a while, he said. He got on well with the owner of the garage, did a good job there. After a while, the owner died, just dropped dead. The family let Gene run the place before deciding to sell the business. When Gene asked the family if they'd let him buy it, he'd pay it off over a long period of time, they wanted money, they needed the cash, and didn't want to wait for it. This was all before the war when so many were struggling, when outlaws picked up sympathy. People were … I don't know. Everything was so upside down for a while.

"I was in a bar on Santa Monica Boulevard," Mary Rose went on, getting around to her first encounter with the man. "It had a funny name. I had been in Los Angeles for some months. I guess I went in alone thinking maybe some movie person would walk in, sweep me off my feet. I wasn't even a fan of the pictures really. But when you're there in Hollywood, and everyone's talking about the picture business, and the people they know, or the people they've met, or saw on the street one time, it gets pretty exciting. It's like falling into a fast-moving river. You're in, and it's moving, and you couldn't stop it if you wanted to. When Gene came in, he talked about one day having his own garage in the Hollywood area. It sounded so sweet and down to earth. Suddenly I felt sorry for all the girls falling for boys who said they were actors or business dealers on the cusp of getting a big job at a big studio. I imagined a future, something sturdy I could depend on. The blue collar, middle class nature of it didn't bother me at all. I guess I just wanted a place to firmly plant my feet … and a nice guy. I had no idea how he planned to afford this garage. I was nineteen. Someone once told me it's easy to get out of a good relationship, but from a bad relationship you can never escape."

Her words made him feel sheltered, inexperienced. He too felt sympathetic toward Gene, though Gene was clearly a bad man. Perhaps Mary Rose's experiences and observations prepared her for this moment. Perhaps hard luck refined her dreams of what a man should be. Eddie didn't know. He considered his own deficiencies, his lack of sophistication. If mistakes paved the way to wisdom, what was she doing with him? Wasn't it only a matter of time before she left, found someone better? What were they to each other anyway, aside from partners in crime?

They passed San Antonio and Houston before finally arriving in Beaumont. It was night and they needed rest. Eddie wished the drive would never end. A voice from somewhere inside spoke ominously about their final stop. In movies, a day of reckoning always arrived. Was life not the same? Maybe it wasn't, and Eddie would come to appreciate reality, where the bad guy gets away sometimes. Probably not, he thought. Good things happened to some people, he knew, but his life had habituated him to lose.

For now, he enjoyed the bridge between where he had been and wherever the road was taking him. He loved driving. Nothing seemed to matter. All he had to do was drive carefully and focus on the road. There were no crucial decisions needed, just miles to cover. How incredible the automobile, he thought, regrettable he never had one. How much happier he might've been, hitting the highways occasionally, leaving his restless energy with the things flashing by.

Weaving through downtown Beaumont, they came upon sizable crowds along the Fannin and Pearl Street sidewalks. They cruised beneath a gleaming in golden light marquee. A picture titled *Foreign Intrigue* was playing, starring Robert Mitchum.

Pointing to a red brick building towering over the theater, Mary Rose said, "Let's get a room at this hotel and see the Robert Mitchum picture."

The idea thrilled Eddie, too tempting to pass up, unbelievable, he thought. The obvious concerns were quickly beaten back by Mary Rose demanding he pull to the curb next to a Sears and wait while she runs inside to buy him a cowboy hat. He did as he was told, unable to resist, and a short while later they rented a fancy room at the Hotel Beaumont.

It was a pleasant night, probably seventy degrees. Stars filled the sky, and *Foreign Intrigue* was a humdinger of a picture. Luxurious European locales, unimaginable wealth, beautiful cars surrounding an unflustered Robert Mitchum mesmerized Eddie. "I didn't like pretending emotion for a man I despised," Genevieve Page purred while looking into Mitchum's eyes, referring to her dead husband. "You loved me once," she went on. "I wanted you. Very much." With the score shifting to a softer melody, Mitchum leaned closer. "I never knew that," he replied.

"Women can hide when they want."

"And so you just stopped wanting?"

"I stopped hiding. I still want. Come with me, Dave."

When the picture ended, they walked to the Carnation Ice Cream Shop. Wearing his cowboy hat mashed above his eyes, no one looked twice at him. Entering, they hit the smell of grilled burgers like a wall. A waitress brought menus, and Eddie couldn't stop talking about the magnificent ornate movie theater, better than The Barstow, he'd never been to a theater where a live organist played before the picture. They each ordered a burger with fries, and Mary Rose said, "I would like to go to another movie tomorrow night."

Back in their room, she talked of Los Angeles. She told stories with excitement for the city she hadn't previously expressed. At times Eddie thought she might be trying to impress him. She seemed to have taken on some of his own characteristics, his own wild-eyed fervor for the glamour and escape of Hollywood, the gods and goddesses up on that beautiful screen.

***

When morning arrived, Eddie's head again felt heavy with questions. He awoke easily but assessed his circumstances with angst. What was he doing here? Were police waiting outside? What were the people of Barstow saying? How was he going to get out of this? What feelings did Mary Rose have for him?

Maybe everything will turn out to be roses and white fences, nighttime strolls for ice cream. Maybe he and Mary Rose could fill their future with adventures and crime stories on the radio and forget all the hand-wringing suspense of the past. Who was he kidding? He was a time bomb, he realized. A bank heist was nothing he'd ever get away with. Seeing himself in jail, he considered that he might find solace in a return to routine, a life among walls. Should he tell Mary Rose what Connie said? She'd hate him if she found out what he'd been keeping from her. Why did his life have to be so complicated?

Sitting on the edge of the bed, he sniffed his armpit, nearly choked on the rancid smell, observed his rumpled, slept-in clothing, the small splotches of dried bloodstains, and stood. Mary Rose stirred. "I'll be right back," Eddie whispered to her. She murmured, kept her eyes closed. Eddie dropped the room key in his pants, returned the cowboy hat to his head, and left.

The morning air touched him gently with its chill. He walked by the Jefferson Theater fresh with memories from a night he knew he'd never forget. At a magazine stand, he bought a newspaper. Sucking in a sharp courageous breath, he rummaged through it. There was an article about bus segregation laws, the Suez crisis but absolutely nothing at all about the heist. He then asked the man behind the register if any clothing shops were open.

"Not for another couple of hours."

Eddie wondered if there were any horrible diseases he could catch from wearing dirty clothes for so long. "I noticed a lot of pretty churches around here."

"Where you from?"

"Cleveland. Passing through."

Returning to the Hotel Beaumont, Eddie felt foolish for walking down the street, taking such risks but also relieved to have seen no pictures of him in the newspapers. Had Connie exaggerated? Maybe all the commotion was local. Switching his thoughts to breakfast ideas, he went upstairs to 309, didn't knock, as he wasn't accustomed to knocking, and entered. Mary Rose, shocked, pulled a towel closer, covering a portion of her wet body. "Oh!" she cried, and then raced across the room, vanishing. Eddie saw much of her, the plump round cheeks of her bottom, the slimness of her waist, her back, her shoulders, and little hands—they had been digging in her purse, probably for cigarettes. Frozen, blood rushing, heart pounding, horrified by his intrusion, his thoughtless action causing such embarrassment, Eddie didn't know what to say. Should he tell her he saw nothing, feign nonchalance? What did she expect him to do? Should he try a joke?

No sound came from the bathroom. Was she dressing? Had she expected him to leave, head sunk in humiliation? He couldn't remove the pictures of her from his mind. He wished he'd seen more. A tingling rushed him, weakened him. He closed his eyes, wobbly from excitement. He wished he could wrap his arms around her. Was this done on purpose? Had she been waiting for him? He saw her naked.

"I'll be right out," she pleasantly called.

"So sorry. I should—"

"It's okay, my fault."

He knelt and untied then tied again his shoes, thinking she might step out, see him engaged in casual activity, and accept his clumsiness as insignificant. He shook his head. Again her magnificent flesh rose to the forefront of his mind. He recalled textbook pictures of paintings housed in European museums, erotic displays of ancient Greek and Roman scenes, radiant female forms proffered like religious experiences. She was so beautiful, a classically proportioned masterpiece.

When she reappeared from the bathroom, she was dressed, as she had been the night before, in white ankle-length narrow pants and a blue sleeveless blouse. She stepped across the carpet in bare feet, not looking at Eddie, brushing her wet hair. Was she pretending nothing happened? "Where did you go?" she asked.

"I went out," Eddie mumbled, "thought a store would be open. I need a shirt, could use one, so ..." What was she thinking? She seemed different from the night before, impatient.

"I was thinking we should go out on our own this morning," she said, finally turning to him.

"For how long?"

"Oh, I don't know. A while. I'd like to get my hair done, pick up a few things. Maybe you shouldn't be seen. If you like, I can buy you new clothes."

Eddie agreed—he would've agreed to anything she wanted—and was soon waiting for her return. He showered, put on the same filthy shirt, and with no television, no radio, no book to read, he sat quietly in a chair, thinking. Why hadn't he knocked? Common courtesies rarely occurred to him. He once found a toy in his yard, knew it belonged to his neighbor's young son, yet rather than give it back he threw it in the garbage. His internal thoughts had always been a friend to him, someone to commiserate with. For years he told himself he didn't need anybody. Had he been rewarded in any way from such conceited delusions? His life was a wreck. He had to let Mary Rose know that law enforcement knew nothing about her, and that she might be smart to get away, leave him to his fate. He'd tell her as soon as she returned. Somehow, he had to be a better man.

**

The air rifling through the Coupe had thickened. Skies were a murky swirl of gray. Eddie's eyes appreciated the diminished brightness. He also felt better in a new shirt. He tried getting around to her involvement in the heist, the police being unaware of her but he rambled, talked about other things while grasping for courage. Could he also have been competing with Gene for her sympathies? Possibly, Eddie thought. He wasn't sure.

"He was a furniture salesman, my dad. He used to mention how most of our neighbors' homes were filled with furniture from his store. Nothing fancy, he sold functional pieces. He was very pragmatic, very practical, my dad. He felt it was important to give people something they needed. 'People need a good bank,' he'd say, 'a place where they can put their money, know it's safe. A good banker can keep track of it, offer advice on how to protect it.' But no matter how hard he sold it, it wasn't something I wanted to do. He wasn't a bad dad. He was a good dad. He had a temper, boy, though, let me tell you. Mostly, he'd unleash on my mother but with me too; I think he had a hard time with my not marrying and giving him grandkids. Maybe he saw some of my mother in me when I was younger … and when I was older, I don't know. They'd have parties and my mom would sometimes start cleaning before the guests left, and it drove my dad crazy, and sometimes she would ask questions and go on and on, interrogating him, never letting up, scrutinizing and questioning every detail of what he said. After a while, he started making things more difficult for her. He'd purposefully leave a mess, knowing it would get on her nerves. I hated it. He could be mean when he wanted to. He was in France at the tail end of The Great War and I think he came back with ideas that everything would be really happy all the time or something. I don't know. He never talked about it much. I had a friend, his name was Lowell, and his father had two families. It's true. He didn't find out until he was fourteen. His dad was a traveling salesman. He was gone all the time. He had another wife and children no one knew about in Oregon. Isn't that something? Lowell never said a bad word about his father though; spoke of him with reverence in fact. Always felt sorry for poor Lowell. I think he's doing fine now though. I don't know."

"Men are stupid," she said simply over the rush of wind.

Eddie felt a little stung by the insult. He'd seen a feisty, impetuous side to her surface over the last couple of days. She hadn't looked at him when she said it. Was she expressing impatience with him? Had he been talking too much? Injecting levity in his voice, a teasing tone, he said, "If you have it all figured out, how did you end up with Gene?"

"You don't have to have it all figured out to know boys are dumb. That's just a basic starting point. It's obvious to everyone on the planet, isn't it? You can know boys are dumb and still know next to nothing about anything else. It's as simple as one, two three."

Thinking it through, he found no argument with her. The image of her nude backside had been flashing through his mind for hours. Mentally, he flipped through pages of a picture book and every picture was identical to the last. He couldn't close the book if he wanted to. Why wasn't he made to be a man who attracts women? His life had been so lonely. Even Gene Green with his stupid name and villainous ways could attract Mary Rose but not Eddie. Why God hands a person four aces and another two pair was a puzzle that could drive one mad.

Rolling through a small residential district, with Lafayette rising out of the earth a few miles ahead, strange clouds like gray whales hovering above, Eddie spotted a boy in a striped shirt, slick hair, and denims, walking along a cracked sidewalk with a stack of newspapers. "Maybe we should see if there's any reporting about ... what happened."

He pulled to the curb, idled, while Mary Rose jumped out and purchased a newspaper from the happy youngster. She returned to the Coupe, opened the paper, turned over a couple of pages, and then said, "Wait a minute. There is something."

She read, and as she read, Eddie felt he was falling. He became dizzy. It couldn't be real, he thought. He was going to be sick. His foolish actions had led to something infinitely worse than he ever could've imagined. It was a nightmare. He looked at the newspaper and didn't want to believe it was a newspaper. The boy wasn't a boy.

According to the article, somewhere in the Arizona desert, Mr. Eugene C. Green was shot in the back of the head at close range. He was shot? How could that be?

Evidence suggested Mr. Green died instantly. The corpse was in a gruesome state resulting from wildlife in the desert attracted to the smell of rapidly decomposing flesh. One set of tire tracks approached and left the scene. No murder weapon was found. Wanted for questioning was Mr. Edward M. Howard, Assistant Manager at the Security Pacific Bank in Barstow. Mr. Howard was also wanted in connection to a heist at the bank that employed him for seventeen years. Authorities believed the murder occurred as a result of greed between co-conspirators as the money stolen from the Barstow bank was not recovered at the execution-style slaying. Also sought for questioning was Marilyn Rose of Los Angeles, daughter of the victim. Where was she? Where was Mr. Howard? How could Mr. Green have been murdered? Police were not forthcoming with everything they knew, yet they insisted the community had been helpful in providing information and the result of which would lead to justice.

Chapter Eight

The happiest people Eddie ever knew were his father's parents. All the time they laughed, and were good at getting laughs. Eddie's grandfather, an Irishman, used his hands to make a living. A fellow could make a fine living back then if he knew how to build something. He'd take a hammer to anything, and afterwards he had something to look at, something to show for his efforts. Things were different back then.

"Do you think they know about the Coupe?" Mary Rose asked.

Eddie was contemplative. Her question barely ruptured his thoughts. He considered how he had always adapted, always found the facility to amble through the motions. He seldom burst with the type of rage that produced any change in his life. He went along with circumstances, always feeling he had no options. He did have options of course, but with the exception of recent actions, he had always chosen the biggest, most visible road available to him. He lacked the courage to explore less obvious roads.

"I don't know," he answered.

"The safe technician was such a big mouth, he probably told them everything."

When Eddie didn't reply, she said, "Lighten up. It's a joke. You're so serious."

"People think we're murderers."

Despite her attempt at levity, Eddie could tell Mary Rose was frightened. Her shoulders hunched; the posture of a woman proud and mindful of her figure had gone. He didn't know what to say. Everything swimming through his head that might offer comfort sounded like a lie.

He imagined prison but couldn't fully imagine it. Prison scenes from movies flashed through his mind, and he was one of the characters. Nothing seemed real. Was he just unlucky, born in the wrong era? Deep down Eddie knew that wasn't right. There was something wrong with him. Something in his blood was different. He was a voyeur, not comfortable living life, making choices; he liked watching others. He was a coward. That was the brutal truth, wasn't it? He was frightened. He didn't want to face the curveballs any pitcher worth his salt would throw at him, and so he never stepped to the plate. He watched others do it.

"Do you think they know about the safe technician?" asked Mary Rose. "Maybe they have him in custody, and maybe he's telling them a story to get himself off the hook."

"I don't know."

"You're not even listening."

East of Baton Rouge, a deep jungle green blanketed the earth. The sky was dense and blinding. Little gas remained in the tank. Around every bend and over every hill Eddie expected a roadblock.

"I wonder if they know we're not in Arizona anymore. They probably already rummaged through the apartment Gene and I had in Los Angeles looking for a photograph of me. Maybe the beauty shop clerk I purchased hair dye from will recognize me, and tell them I have black hair now. My God, anything could happen, so many ways things could unravel."

"If they think we did it," Eddie reasoned out loud, "then it's likely they know nothing about the safe technician, whatever his name is, which means they wouldn't know about the Coupe."

"We should keep the car?"

"No. Better to be safe."

"I guess so. I wonder if the radio has talked about what we look like. Surely, plenty of people have offered descriptions to the police. Even if there isn't a recent

photograph of you, people know what you look like, and all
those people will talk."

"Ever been to Baton Rouge?"

"No."

"We should get a new car here. We're taking on
greater risk if we don't."

"What do we do with this one?"

"Leave it. Doesn't matter. What else could we do
with it?"

When they arrived in the city, Eddie pulled to the
curb at a phone booth. Mary Rose jumped out, her heels
tapping concrete. A dilapidated Meat Market and Soda
Shop had a few customers, blacks, coming and going. He
hadn't been used to seeing so many. He met the anger and
suspicion in their eyes by turning away from them. Inside
the booth, Mary Rose ripped a page from a phone book.
She plugged the phone with a coin and dialed. She spoke
with someone. Eddie marveled at the way she moved. She
looked like Ava Gardner only softer. Even while anxious,
she was painfully beautiful.

A short time later, several long blocks deeper into
the city, Eddie was again alone in the car, waiting for Mary
Rose. Needing to remain out of sight, he parked ten
minutes from a used car lot. Mary Rose had thumbed off
eight hundred dollars from their stash, told him it may take
a while, not to get impatient, she'd return with an
automobile. He waited for what must've been two hours.

He'd given the radio stations a few minutes, closed
his eyes for a while, told his heart to slow down, and his
head to adopt a stoic demeanor. He imagined being lost in
the Sahara, enemies with the sun above. Where was she?
What could possibly be taking so long? A hundred times he
thought of driving past the car lot to see if he could see her,
make sure she was still there. He held back. What if she
wasn't there? Losing her would be the loss of everything.

She had told him it could take a while. She knew he'd get impatient. She knew him well, better than he knew her.

Finally, she parked beside him in a 1940 Ford Deluxe. Eddie grabbed the sacks of cash, and raced into the passenger seat of their new vehicle. Mary Rose must've gotten directions from the dealer, as she quickly and confidently burned up a network of turns to get them back on the freeway. They launched out of Baton Rouge, heading further east, the wind whipping around their faces again. A mid-day Louisiana sun caressed their new machine's black lacquer. It was a splendid purchase. The inside had wood-grained molding. The dash on the Deluxe was sleek with art deco typeface beneath measurements for speed, oil pressure, temperature, and fuel. It may have been an older car, but had been exceedingly well kept.

"What're you thinking about?" Eddie asked, noticing she had been quiet.

She shrugged, lit a cigarette, and answered, "Just trying to think of ways to disappear."

"What took so long?"

"I was buying a car, Eddie. It's not like buying a pack of gum."

Gulfport Mississippi was one hundred and twenty miles further on. After that would be Alabama and then Florida. What waited up ahead? Eddie wondered. Had investigators cast a wider net, expanded beyond the west? What would Detective Joe Friday do?

Something changed in Mary Rose. Her mood fell. She wasn't trying to be funny anymore. She sounded miserable when she said she wanted to disappear. Eddie knew she was frightened. This was different. Her eyes were unblinking, focused on something a thousand miles away.

"You did a good job getting this car," he told her.

He received no acknowledgment, and so he approached a topic that had been on his mind since the night of the heist. "I've been thinking. I'm curious about something. I wanted to ask you something. Are you listening?"

"Of course."

He let a mile or so pass, unsure, and then said, "You were different before."

"What do you mean?"

"I don't know. Different."

"I wasn't wanted for murder," she snapped. "I wasn't running from the law."

"I guess I shouldn't have brought it up."

"It's a stupid question." As Eddie stared through the unblemished windshield, saying nothing, Mary Rose's defensiveness intensified. "The man I've been living with, gave my life to, these last couple of years has been killed. You don't think that does something to a person? On top of that, I'm one of the accused. The police think I did it."

"Your voice was even different."

"My voice was the same."

"No, you were more ... I don't know ... womanly. Not that there's anything wrong with you now. I'm just saying, you were a little more ... You smiled a lot."

Angered, Mary Rose raised her volume. "Are you fucking serious?"

"Well, you can say you weren't running from the law back then but you were plotting a bank heist." Eddie's frustration met with hers, erupting in a flurry of hand gestures and rising decibels. "How do you flirt and wiggle around town and act so ... I don't know ... carefree about everything when you're with some guy who's pushing you to rob a bank?"

"Jesus, Eddie! You scrutinize everything too much. Every little thing you dissect it, and question it. I'm the same fucking person, Eddie."

"See? That's what I mean. You never used words like that when we first met."

"Oh, I never used words like that? Known me my whole life, have you?"

"No, I guess I'm wrong. I guess I don't know you at all."

***

Twelve hours had passed since they started the day in the Coupe. Eddie now drove the Deluxe. Mary Rose needed a rest, but she wasn't sleeping. Headlights gave them thirty feet of rushing concrete. Everything else was black, not a black filled with the relief of a beautiful moon and stars, but a murky black as when rain contemplates whether it wants to fall.

They seemed alone in the world until headlights, hungry, eager for their prey, swooped into Eddie's rearview. They hung, agitated, lingering off the back bumper. Who was it? Finally, switching lanes, the vehicle passed. Once it did so, decals and lettering revealed a state trooper. Had the dealer recognized Mary Rose? Were cops killing time, waiting for them, swarming around them? Why not just pull them over?

Eddie tried not to get jumpy. They'd made it to Florida. They'd be in Miami in the morning. If they could manage to get airline tickets, they could be in Cuba as early as noon, staying in a lavish hotel. They'd never return to America. It was bizarre to contemplate—the country of their birth, gone. It was dreamlike and frightening. How had all this come to be?

"They can't identify a person who has no fingerprints," Mary Rose stated after a prolonged silence. "Maybe we should, I don't know, burn our fingerprints off."

"What are you talking about?"

"I'm trying to figure out how we can say we're not who they say we are."

"People who know us could still identify us."

"But I think legally they can't prove it's you without a fingerprint match," she stated definitively before adding as an afterthought, "I'd hate to burn my hands though."

"If my sister saw me in a courtroom she'd say, 'that's my brother except for some reason he set his hands on fire.'"

"Well, we have to think of something."

Eddie let another couple of coal-black miles pass, and then said, "Whatever we do is a long shot. It's against the odds. We have to accept there's no plan out there offering certainty. Most likely, it seems to me, though I hope I'm wrong, we're going to get caught. That's just the way it is. So, I think we have to be willing to consider crazy ideas. Burning fingerprints is an idea, a good one, an okay one. Keep them coming. We have to keep the wheels spinning. I unfortunately don't think that one will work, but I'm open to anything. Meanwhile, I have an idea, while you're working on more, and you're going to think it's crazy, but it just might be crazy enough to be something."

"What is it?"

"Well, I once read about this little town in the Tampa area where there are a lot of mobsters."

"Mobsters? Eddie, are you crazy?"

"I told you, it's an insane idea but think about it. These guys are well connected in Cuba. We tell them we'd like new driver's licenses, different names. We tell them we're prepared to pay a lot of money."

"How much money?"

"I don't know. Five-hundred dollars."

"Just for driver's licenses?"

"Right, then we purchase airplane tickets under new names."

"How're we going to meet mobsters? You can't just go around asking people if they're in the mafia."

"I haven't figured that out yet."

Mocking him, Mary Rose said, "Maybe they're listed in the phone book."

"You're right. We'll just set our hands on fire. That's a much better idea."

She simmered, apparently not liking sarcasm in return, and then said, "Do you know about the Amish?"

"The Amish?"

"They're people who live apart from the rest of us."

"I know who the Amish are. They make furniture and stuff. I've heard of them. Why?"

"I think it's because of their religion they don't drive cars. They don't have driver's licenses. What if we say we're Amish but left. We didn't want to be Amish anymore, and now we need driver's licenses? We can make up whatever names we want."

"Won't they check? There must be some way to verify that you've come from an Amish community."

"How would they do that?"

"I don't know," Eddie said. "What if they ask me to build a table or something? I don't know how to build a table."

"Tell them you did a poor job as an Amish and that's why you're leaving the community."

"Don't we have to be in uniforms or something?"

"You said you wanted crazy ideas."

"No, it's good. I like it. It might be worth a try. I don't know."

Rain started. Eddie rolled up his window, leaving it cracked for the rushing air and the smell of rainwater drizzling down from the black sky. Mary Rose was no longer wearing her perfume, he realized, and he wondered about it. Too embarrassed to mention it, he instead said, "If everything changes, and our lives are never the same again, we're going to forever think of our lives as having two halves, one before all this and one after—"

"I think that's already the case, Eddie."

"I guess so but what I'm wondering is, what'll you remember the most from your previous life?"

She smiled a little. The question seemed to surprise her. Eddie hoped it would diminish the sliver of hostility he felt between them. To his relief, when she answered, her words came with a softer tone. "Oh, I don't know," she said. "I'd really have to think about that one."

"Come on, there has to be something that stands out."

"Mostly grief, running away, not a lot of good memories, Eddie."

"Not even when you were little?"

She looked at him for a moment with a face not easily read. After she turned away, an arm went up, rested on the door, her fingers fluttering, rings tapping the window, and she said, "Once a year, usually around the holidays, Christmas, right around this time of year, I'd spend a weekend with my dad's sister. She wasn't married, had no kids. My aunt would take me shopping in Wichita, buy me a new dress, a piece of jewelry, and then she'd take me out to dinner, always ordering me a milkshake."

"That sounds fun."

"When I was fifteen, she said the door was always open for me to live with her. It was the first I realized there could be a world without my parents. The suggestion alone was liberating. I went home feeling empowered, and it was that event that gave me the courage to leave home a year later. It was a moment that meant a lot to me. I would love to see her again."

Rain intensified. Thunder rumbled. Eddie clicked on his windshield wipers, and closed the crack of rushing air. Her willingness to confide made Eddie feel special. There were traumas she kept to herself, he knew. He wished to learn everything about her, but he wouldn't pry. The heavy clattering of rain was the only sound for a while.

"What about you?" she eventually asked.

"Me? Oh, I have … the standard stuff, presents under the Christmas tree. Boring stuff, really."

"But there must be an extra special moment or you wouldn't have asked me."

Eddie shrugged and shook his head, until she insisted lightheartedly, "Come on, tell," and so he took a breath, and said, "That night we went out to the desert."

"You and me?"

"Yeah. Under the stars."

"Really?"

"Yeah."

"Why?"

"I don't know."

"Yes, you do."

"I guess …. in my head it was like we were together."

"We were together," she stated factually.

"I mean really together, a romantic type of together, together like Rudy Valentino and Vilma Banky, you know, in love."

"Eddie ..."

"It was the closest I've ever felt to something like that."

"Eddie ..."

"No, you don't have to say anything. It's probably best if you don't."

Chapter Nine

Dimly lit at four in the morning was Ybor City, on the northeast side of Tampa. Brick buildings with wrought iron balconies flanked Seventh Avenue, the heart of the area. Eddie and Mary Rose were exhausted, brain dead, stale, feeling they'd been without sleep for days. Though too tired to talk, they briefly mentioned breakfast, the desire for pancakes and eggs and coffee, before falling into silence again.

The morning air was damp and cool. Streetlamps illuminated roving mists. The smell wasn't salty from the sea, but it had a sweet pungency, something unique about it Eddie couldn't quite place.

A number of structures swept past while they scanned for a motel with vacancies. Dazed from indecision and nothing inviting, they kept driving. Eddie had read about Ybor City. He kept bleary eyes to the sidewalks looking for mobsters but the streets were dead. Eventually they passed through Tampa, brilliantly lit in splashy neon even well past midnight. In spite of his fatigue, Eddie found it exciting. "We have to stop and get some sleep," Eddie said. To which, Mary Rose, shadowed except the warmly lit front of her face, nodded.

West of the city, they found a room at the Tahitian Inn. Mary Rose paid the rental, making reference to her "father" in the car worried about luggage being left alone. The attendant, an elderly woman, couldn't have been less interested. Eddie shoved the paper sacks of cash under the bed once they got into their room. Mary Rose told Eddie she would take a fast shower before going to sleep. With the sound of the shower droning near to him, Eddie sat astonished on the edge of the bed, hands flat against a soft gold-colored and smoothly stretched blanket. How did he get here? It all happened so fast. In a few days, he'd arrived at the other side of the country. To him it felt as far as the other side of the moon.

He hadn't said anything to Mary Rose about it yet, but he figured their only chance of escape was the mob. In order to swindle driver's license examiners, they not only had to convince the issuing authority to believe whatever ridiculousness they came up with, but also had to pass tests on vision; read and understand traffic signs, and pass tests on safety and traffic laws. That meant they had to fool a number of people. If they succeeded in all that, they would then wait days, maybe even weeks for driver's licenses to arrive by mail, and what address would they give? They didn't have the luxury of days. A murderer was running free. Law enforcement would act tirelessly, chasing every lead, no matter how small until the job was finished.

Eddie stood from the bed and paced, tried to loosen the pressure welling in his head. On each side of the bed were ceramic lamps made to look like carved tiki statues. The furniture was framed in fake bamboo. What an odd room, he thought. It might've been funny under different circumstances. On a desk were two Polynesian girls roughly the size of Christmas ornaments or salt and peppershakers, but Eddie couldn't comprehend the purpose for them. What mysterious things they were, he pondered. Why would anyone want them?

"What's wrong?" Mary Rose stood wrapped in white towels, the bathroom light framing her from behind.

Eddie considered revealing his troubled thoughts but it was nearly dawn, and they were both worn-out. He sat on the bed again, and muttered, "I guess I'm just hoping we get through this."

She approached. She sat next to him, and placed a hand on his shoulder. "One thing at a time, Eddie." She then squeezed muscles in his neck, gently, lovingly clawed fingernails all over his back, and added, "We have to sleep."

Her touch had him falling to pieces inside. Eddie felt delirious. What was she thinking? Was she thinking about what he said earlier? Were her affections the result of pity?

She kissed his shoulder. Her hand moved to his head. Fingers combed through his hair. "Go to sleep," she whispered. "Everything's going to be fine." She crouched down in front of him, untied his shoes, and pulled them off his feet. She stood then, and let out a giggle before his slumped form. "Eddie, go to sleep." Her little palm went to his forehead and playfully shoved him back onto the bed.

***

The Ybor City sky was blue, crowded with white tuffs and gray rain. Streets were busy, shaded in spots, and brightly lit elsewhere. Was it a Saturday? Cafes were crowded too, too crowded for a workday. What day was it? Eddie had no idea. One place looked like an atrium, packed with eaters in colorful clothes, sipping coffees from small cups, conversing in loud warbles, telling stories. Men wore white suits. Cigars were smoked. For a moment, Eddie watched from a sidewalk. They should be in there, he thought, enjoying time together, having a normal day. They'd had a hearty breakfast. Mary Rose fetched it from somewhere and brought it to their room at the Tahitian. While satisfying their starved stomachs with eggs, bacon and buttered toast, Eddie informed her of his plans for the afternoon. He would go alone in case he was picked up, told her if he's not back by the next morning, she should take the money and go, maybe backtrack, make her way to Mexico or head north to Canada, maybe bribe her way onto a boat and sail to the other side of the world. She said little. At one point her eyes focused again on something a thousand miles away, and he said, "If I don't make it, don't worry about me," and she replied, "Don't be dramatic."

That was all she said. "Don't be dramatic." Such a mysterious woman, Eddie reflected. What had horrified her in her youth, made her resentful of her parents? What would her family say about her? Did she have siblings? There was something quirky about her, and whatever it was, he believed he would eventually find it relatable. Her unpredictable nature made her appealing to Eddie nearly beyond her movie-goddess looks.

A cab had dropped him off on Seventh Avenue, and as he walked without her, he missed her. Loneliness bit his heart. He shook off a surprising swell of tears as he started along the sidewalk. A moment later, he made his eyelids hang heavy and turned his jaw to stone as he thought of Robert Mitchum. Could he pretend to be someone else, someone more courageous? Before another five steps, the pose slipped away. He was no Mitchum or Bogart. Who was he kidding? They were tough guys. He was something different, a guy they didn't make films about.

Apprehensive, Eddie considered the task before him. He had a plan. He would approach a bartender, and then ask where he could get in touch with a mobster while placing an irresistible tip on the bar. Mary Rose had expressed her fears once she heard the plan, even said they're smarter than him, but he explained the dilemma, the lack of choice as he saw it, and her objections ended. He had put it to her plainly, and she understood.

Walking at a good pace now, wishing he had his glasses so he could see into the eyes of those around him, Eddie thought of the conversation from the night before when he essentially admitted to her his feelings. Should he not have said anything? Deep down, he knew this was the end of the road. He couldn't stop thinking that if she only loved him he'd accept his fate. It would be like the ending of a movie, the climax of a tragic love affair.

Everything was moving so fast. Yet it seemed far more than three nights had passed since they were in Marfa. Much had happened since then—the affection she showed the night before, for example. He thought back to when he was little, and for a time pleaded with his mother every day for a haircut. A neighbor woman routinely cut his hair for a nickel. Mom and Dad worried something was wrong with Eddie when he began demanding a haircut every day. One day, Dad threw a fit. "That boy is not the one in control of this household!" Eddie's simple reasoning, though he couldn't articulate it, was that he loved having the neighbor lady touch his hair, run a comb over his head, the way she would delicately pull a clump of hair with two fingers and snip a straight line with her scissors. She never spoke to him, never asked him about school, or pressed him about sports. She wore a pretty dress, and her arms smelled good, and sometimes she'd bump against him with her hips. In some ways, Mary Rose reminded him of that great woman.

Eddie had been walking for some time. A few blocks from Seventh Avenue, he spotted The Yellow House Bar. Entering, he cautiously checked his back. The bar was dark inside, difficult to see, and the darkness stole a few breathless moments. What was this place? Who was watching him? Was this the bar he should try? Did it seem like a place with mobster connections? Perry Como's mid-40's hit *Prisoner of Love* sang from a jukebox. A man in a corner spoke loudly in a language Eddie didn't understand. Gaining clarity, Eddie stepped to the bar. The man behind it had a heavy round face hanging beneath a narrow forehead. His nose was thick and rough. Small eyes aimed high, giving him the appearance of one who musters an effort to think.

"I'll have a bottle of beer," Eddie said, and the big man who looked to be in his fifties quickly set one before him.

"Been here a while?" Eddie asked.

The man sneered while answering, "Me or the joint?"

"You. You from around here?"

"Who's asking?"

"Uh … my name's Paul. I'm down from Cleveland. Never been here before."

The man nodded and walked away without answering the question. Eddie pivoted on his stool, his vision pretty good now, and saw a number of customers, mostly loners, and one with an opened newspaper in his hands.

Returned to facing the bar, Eddie sipped his beer. The bartender raised a lit cigar from an ashtray, replacing the thin line of smoke from the tip into a cloud as he puffed on it. What if he failed to get a contact from the guy? There was a great temptation to leave, think up some other plan, but other plans were more problematic, and time was running out.

"Nice town," Eddie said to the bartender, reaching out for some attention. Earning no response, he then said, "You don't have some issue with me being here, do you?"

The big man ambled back to Eddie, keeping his cigar between fat fingers. He sighed and mangled his droopy face before replying, "I'm sorry. Most people like to come in here, drink, eat some lunch, and be left alone. What do you want?"

"Friendly conversation."

"About what?"

Removing a five-dollar bill from his pocket, Eddie placed it on the bar, leaned in so others couldn't hear, and said, "Look, I know some people who got themselves into some problems. These aren't the kind of problems police can help with. I was informed there might be people around here who could help."

"Informed by who?" the man asked.

Eddie's breath caught. "Well, it was … I didn't actually know … I read somewhere, a story, an article in a newspaper. This is a popular area for people who … uh … work outside the system."

"I don't know what you're talking about."

Eddie looked at the five-dollar bill, unsure what to say as the big man snatched it with no expression of gratitude. "I can give you more," Eddie said after a moment.

The bartender shot his eyes over Eddie's head, and then leered at him, saying, "I don't know what you want."

"I'm not a cop or anything like that. I'm simply asking for your help. Point me in the right direction. You can't get in trouble for that. I'm tipping you for a drink. I'll gladly tip you for another if that's what you want."

"I think you've come to the wrong place."

"What would be the right place? I've got money for help, and I've got money for a big favor."

"What favor?"

"Well, how do I know I'm talking to the right guy?"

"You seem like a clown. You want a drink; I'll let you drink. If there's something else you want I don't have it."

Eddie left. He didn't know what to do, where to go. He thought back to a conversation with Mary Rose. She'd affectionately spoken of a dog she had when she was a little girl. "I would bend down on my knees and pull his paws up onto my shoulders. He was huge, and his mouth was always hanging open, slobbering all over, and I'd pretend he was giving me a big hug. I loved that big furry chest of his, and I'd nestle my face into the folds of his neck. I could do anything with that guy. He was pure sweetness. Someday I want to have another dog."

Eddie saw a boy selling newspapers. Did the newspapers have a story about the bank heist? Were the cops closing in? Eddie fished a dime from a pocket, and called to the boy. Once he had the newspaper in his hands, he began to think the boy might know someone. Why wouldn't he? He spent his days on the streets, watching the same people come and go. He'd hear things. "You like money?" he asked the boy.

A white smile beamed from copper-colored skin. He looked between eight and ten years old. Large slacks looked like they were cut with a scissors at the bottom. His shirt was also too big. Suspenders provided at least some dignity.

"You know people in the neighborhood, right?" Eddie kneeled and gave the boy five dollars. He saw the boy's dark chocolate eyes widen with excitement, and so he revealed another five dollars. "I'll give you ten dollars for some help. Will you help me?" Off the boy's nod, Eddie continued. "I want you to understand something though. I'm not a cop. I'm not with the police. I'm looking for someone who can do me a favor."

"What favor?" the boy asked.

"That's not important to the business between you and me. What I need from you is to find me the guy."

"What's he look like?"

"I'm not sure. He'd be a guy who walks around a lot while other men are at work. He'd be a tough looking guy, maybe. You might've seen police hassling him."

"He does things illegal?"

"That would be him."

A short while later, the boy pointed at Eddie from a block away while a stocky man followed the finger's aim from over slim shoulders. Something was said between the two, and then the man crossed the street, marching toward Eddie with an elongated confident gait. He had thick dark hair, maybe an inch of forehead. Approaching Eddie, he impatiently asked, "Who are you?"

Eddie momentarily fell back on his heels before responding, "Who are you?"

"The boy said you're looking for someone. Who are you looking for? What do you want?"

Hours were flying by, pressuring Eddie to risk his life with a stranger. In a flash, he imagined being hauled somewhere, held for a ransom the stranger hoped Mary Rose might pay. He wouldn't give up her name or location, though, no matter what. He'd take his poison and be done with the world.

Impatience tightened the man's face, and so Eddie muttered, "I'm just an average guy, you see, but I got into some trouble. I need help."

Eyeballs scrutinized, probing deeper, prompting Eddie to hang his face with as much transparency as he could. "I'm not a cop. I'm not working for any commission of the congress or anything like that."

A sharp chin lifted. "Follow me," the stranger said. He walked in front of Eddie, and Eddie saw his gaze dart in all directions, a brief second to one side before switching to another. He moved fast, charging with a brisk extended stride. Eddie felt confident they were walking in a westerly direction. At Fifteenth Street, they swung right, rounding the Las Novedadez restaurant. After three blocks, they turned again before slipping into a narrow alley.

Seconds later, they were surrounded by four brick walls. The tops of palms peered over buildings, watching like the faces of children in a thunderstorm. Trashcans were stuffed. Grease puddles wet the concrete. A bicycle leaned against a wall with sun-baked and cracked flattened tires. Nerves became a noose around Eddie's chest, strangling his pounding heart. It seemed a suitable place for a life to end violently and mysteriously.

"Give me your wallet," the stranger demanded.

"What for?" Eddie asked.

"I thought I heard a man who had run out of options. I don't know what I can do for you but I'm not doing anything without your wallet first."

Eddie reached around to his back pocket while asking, "Do you just want the money I'm holding? I don't have much on me."

"Give me the whole thing."

The stranger rummaged through the wallet quickly, without expression, and then said to Eddie, "Wait here and I'll be back. Don't go nowhere. Leave this spot and we're done. Can you follow that? It's very simple. Don't go nowhere," he repeated. "Wait here."

"You'll help me?"

"Wait here." With Eddie's wallet jammed in a pocket, the stranger left.

Would he ever come back? Eddie wondered. Had he just idiotically worsened his circumstances? He didn't even have cab fare to get back to the Tahitian. He thought about Mary Rose. It had been hours since he left her. Was she still there, awaiting his return, or had she taken the Deluxe and the money and gone? He thought about the sickly safe technician. Why did he kill Gene Green? Where was he now? Was he finished with Eddie and Mary Rose or would he pursue them for the stolen money?

A maddening amount of time passed. Soon the old bricks seemed to close in with the coming darkness. Eddie paced. His feet hurt. He wanted to sit, but the ground was filthy. Twilight painted the palm trees orange. Eddie watched with nothing to do but think. He considered how every second of every day somewhere on Earth something was ending. The sun was waning, someone was dying—a relentless consistency of endings. Not long after that there was a smattering of stars among blackness. The warm bricks touched by his hands turned cold. Palm trees became silhouettes, swaying, tugged by a light breeze, having lost all interest in him. How horrible knowing so little, he thought. Eddie felt he'd been moving toward some destination; he didn't know what, but believed it might offer the chance to look back with deference and even some appreciation for all the twists and turns. Instead, he had darkness and knew nothing. Stabbed by emptiness and doubt, despite years of loneliness to draw from, Eddie never felt such isolation, never felt so detached from everything. Maybe this was planned. Maybe this was what he was supposed to feel at death's door.

***

Eddie didn't want to offend by checking to see if the cash he had been carrying remained when the stranger returned and gave Eddie his wallet back. He simply tucked it into a pocket. The stocky, energetic man looked no different from many hours earlier. He stood in one spot yet with a flurry of movements. Eyes flew over his shoulders. He jerked and twitched like a fish on dry land.

"Let's go," he said, and Eddie followed. "Make it fast."

From the alley, they emerged onto the sidewalk, passing women in sultry dresses, hands under the arms of men in suits. Cigarettes and cigars were smoked. Faces carried the smiles of indulgences met—rich foods, drinking, perhaps more. The stranger stopped after two blocks at a door, pivoting in a half circle toward the street, putting eyes to everything before entering. Up a flight of stairs he went, down a hallway, until at another door, number 26, he knocked.

"Let him in," a voice called from inside.

The man Eddie had been following opened the door and gestured with a head nod for Eddie to enter. What was he getting into? None of this was anything like what Eddie had anticipated. He had imagined great packs of men, lounging, talking loudly, all deferential to one most mysterious and dangerous figure who provided counsel on even the smallest decision.

A man with a square face and large glasses sat behind a desk. He was alone. Hands were flattened on the desk, and glowed dazzlingly bright from a small lamp.

Shadows stole everything else, creating a sinister view. The door behind Eddie shut, and his escort was gone, although Eddie heard no footsteps. The man stood from behind the desk, his face dimming to complete darkness while the window at his back permitted some light from the street below.

The man spoke slowly, confidently, and Eddie thought he detected some age, a roughness in the voice. "I know who you are, and I know what you did," he said.

"What did I do?"

He fished a cigarette pack from a pocket, drummed it into a palm, and pressed one to his lips. Snapping open a lighter, he put fire to his face. Exhaling a long plume of smoke, he said, "Friends call me The Colonel."

"I'd like to be friends," Eddie responded tightly.

He rounded the desk, and as the office was small, Eddie felt the man's closer presence as a somewhat threatening thing. "What exactly are you hoping I might be able to do for you?"

"Very simple … at least I hope … I don't know … I need two identification cards. I'm … um … looking to get out of the country. There are two of us. No one can know."

"An excellent craftsman costs money."

"I have money."

"Tell me about the woman."

"Woman?"

"I told you I know who you are. If you want my help, you won't question what I say."

Eddie knew he was mentally out-gunned. He'd never come close to a situation like this before. The Colonel knew people, had far-reaching connections, and had spent a lifetime twisting arms to his advantage. "She's a friend," Eddie answered.

"She's very beautiful."

Eddie swallowed hard. "You saw a photo?"

A hand gripped The Colonel's jaw, rubbed thoughtfully, and then fell away while another hand lifted the cigarette again to his lips. "You marrying her?"

"Why?"

"You should marry her. Do you love her? I assume you must but even if you don't, you should marry her. Marriage is good. Children are good."

"Excuse me, sir ... Colonel ... if I may, what does that have to do with anything?"

"It's important. A man should have a family. Without a family, a man cares only for himself, and that's not good. In time, a man loses strength. It's inevitable. If he cares only for himself and loses strength, he has only his weakness to consider, and it's depressing, but when a man with a family becomes weak, he can focus on those who are still strong. Children, grandchildren, and even great grandchildren, if a man is lucky enough, all of these children revitalize a man, remind him of youth."

Unsure what was expected, Eddie nodded and said, "Well, that's true, I'm sure."

"You should have a family. A man your age should already have three children."

"I don't know why we're talking about this."

"You wish to talk business."

"The woman is waiting—"

"Mary Rose."

Eddie's eyes fell away from the darkened face before him. He felt suddenly imprisoned by the opposite side of the law. How had this man come to know so much? "Right," he answered. "She's expecting me. If I don't get there soon, she's leaving. She'll take the money with her. I'll have nothing for myself, and more importantly to this discussion, I'll have nothing I can offer to you."

"I've examined your situation carefully," The Colonel said, and the rough confidence took on a note of ruthlessness. "Your needs weren't hard to figure out. I will have a taxi for your return. I will cover the cost. I will arrange for photos tomorrow. Identification cards will be completed in the evening. I will arrange air travel to wherever you wish to go. I will even have two suitcases purchased so that you will travel more inconspicuously."

Eddie felt his heart thumping. The assurances and certainty and detailed planning elevated him, gave him buoyancy, a sense that he wasn't completely devoid of clever thinking. He'd come to the right place. Yet something in the voice of the man nagged at his newfound refuge.

"How much money came from the bank in Barstow?"

With a hesitant shrug, Eddie answered, "Not much."

"I wish to know the amount."

Eddie wrestled with the answer. Was it possible The Colonel already knew? If he lied, the whole thing could be blown. The Colonel could decide not to trust him. On the other hand, what if The Colonel demanded a huge portion of it? Eddie had anticipated the cost to be hundreds of dollars; what if he wanted thousands? The important thing was to leave this nightmare behind, Eddie reminded himself. "Forty-eight thousand dollars," he said.

"Forty-eight thousand?"

"Yes."

"No more?"

"Forty-eight thousand. That's it. We spent eight hundred on a Ford Deluxe, another couple of hundred traveling."

"Then that is the price you will pay to me."

"What?"

"Two identification cards plus the other items I mentioned will cost you forty-seven thousand dollars. And, Edward, you're not talking to a man who negotiates with people like you. Forty-seven thousand. Life …" he shrugged. "It's expensive."

Chapter Ten

It was late when Eddie returned to the Tahitian. He was exhausted. In the cab, paid for as promised, Eddie wondered how Mary Rose would react to his forfeiting the entire fortune from the heist in order to escape. The total, after all, was not his to negotiate. He knew she would argue, she would insist there must be another way. She was like that. Standing outside the room, the Deluxe visible in the parking lot, Eddie rubbed his head, tired of the beatings he'd been taking for days. Having only hours left seemed unreal. Anything could happen. Would he ever experience another carefree moment?

For perhaps the hundredth time, he itemized the steps they needed to take. He decided not to tell Mary Rose about the money, reasoning that the captain of the ship didn't need a mutiny. He hoped, in the end, her gratitude for keeping them out of jail would be enough to counterbalance the loss of the money. After unlocking the door, he entered darkness. A light went on. She was on the bed, awake, dressed, not even under the sheets, waiting for him. "Eddie," she cried. She hurried to him in bare feet. "I was worried." A delicate hand caressed his arm. Her eyes were red. Had she been crying? "I was so worried. It's late. Is everything okay? I've been just sitting in here thinking how bad everything is. I couldn't stop worrying. I couldn't block out the bad thoughts. Oh, how did we get into this mess? I've been thinking, Eddie, maybe we should go to church. They're open. We could confess the horrible things we've done. I want to ask for forgiveness."

"They have churches in Havana."

"You were able to arrange a departure?"

"Everything's set."

"That's good. Oh, my heart is racing, Eddie. I was so worried." Her face softened, and then brightened with tenderness. "You did good."

"I'm tired."

"Of course, you need rest. How much money do they want?"

"I was able to work it out. It's fine."

"Five hundred dollars?"

Eyes drifting, Eddie answered, "Yeah, it was no problem." He sat on the bed and she stood over him running long fingernails over his back and shoulders. He'd played his cards as well as he could, he told himself. The important thing was to survive and keep Mary Rose safe. He tried to imagine the end of this, tried even harder to see the two of them still spending time together when this was all over. He debated telling her how he felt about her.

A voice told him they wouldn't make it, they'd never get through the airport, a horrible betrayal was just around the corner, and it seemed the voice wasn't finished with him yet. Had the deal been too easy? Eddie knew The Colonel made his way in the world preying on people.

Should he tell her? Did he really want the intensity of his feelings for Mary Rose to remain hidden? Wouldn't he feel better having told her of his affection? He'd hinted at feelings before, but he hadn't really come clean about the degree to which he felt overwhelmed by her nearness, her touch, how his brain seemed to vanish into thin air while the rest of him trembled with heightened sensitivity.

"Do you trust him?" she asked.

"It's our only option."

"You trusted Gene."

It had been his greatest failing. Why had she hit him with it? Maybe it wasn't his greatest failing, he considered. Maybe it wasn't a failing at all. Maybe trusting Gene Green was the best thing he ever did. He wasn't sure. Maybe trusting Gene Green was something he was forced into as a result of worse mistakes? Silence and caution and fear had strangled his life's potential. Why was he silent now?

"Does he know how much money we have?" she asked.

Eddie stood and paced. Such distance from his normal life, future days suddenly emptied of anything remotely familiar, intense feelings for an unpredictable woman; how did he get here? These were terrifying things.

"Eddie, what's wrong?"

"Nothing. Everything's fine."

"You look like you could use some sleep."

Eddie knew he wouldn't sleep. He'd lie still, worried about everything, feeling like he had a bucket of baseballs in his belly. Maybe they should've turned themselves in once they heard about the murder. Running from a murder charge influenced appearances, and weren't appearances all that mattered?

Maybe things would be different someplace else. What promises did the rising sun over Cuba hold? Could he be someone different someplace new? Could Mary Rose develop romantic feelings for him if he successfully facilitated their escape? He closed his eyes and thought about how he'd had enough of days that would dramatically change the course of his future.

When Eddie opened his eyes again, he saw that Mary Rose had shaken off her emotion. She told Eddie to be sure to get some sleep, and then she put herself to bed. She was nothing like his mother, he thought, and then considered how strange for that to be good.

***

She returned with breakfast, just as she had done the day before. Eddie ate little, mostly starred and picked at it. Sleep calmed Mary Rose. She asked nothing further about the money. She seemed good, pleased to be on the verge of a new life. She smoked, bounced around the room, tossing questions, her head obviously spinning with various ways to close the bridge at their backs. He still hadn't worked out how he would hand over all the money without her knowing.

Standing from the bed, Eddie parted thick curtains. The Florida sun took over the room, and he felt ugly in the dazzling brightness. Outside was a pool, white quivers shimmering in a deep blue luster, reminding him of The Town & Country. Kids splashed, climbed out, and dropped back in again. He thought of his peanut butter sandwich and favorite bench across from Harold B. Seton Elementary. Could he start life over? Perhaps it had all been chiseled in stone long ago for some unknowable purpose.

"If anything happens," he said. "If we get caught—"

"What makes you think we'll get caught?"

"We won't. I don't think that," he lied. "I'm just saying that if it does happen, I want you to accuse me, tell the police I was behind it. I made the decisions. You didn't want to go along with it. I forced you. Whatever you accuse me of I'll back you up. If the worst happens, we'll make sure you go free."

Her voice, fragile sounding, called from behind. "Eddie …" He turned a questioning face. She continued, "I'm sorry if I got you into something you regret."

"Everything happened so fast," Eddie replied. "I wish we could slow it down. I wish we had time to … I don't know."

He wanted to wrap her in his arms but he couldn't move. Romantic scenes from films played in his mind. It was enough to be in her presence, he told himself. He had no regrets. He was lucky. He looked at her and offered a fast smile. She nodded, and then she left, said she needed more cigarettes.

Again, Eddie went over the plan. He reminded himself of the need to remain focused. It was not easy. Everything visible seemed to shiver in time with his pounding heart. He breathed with difficulty. Perhaps a shower would do him some good, he thought. He should have eaten before his breakfast turned cold.

A moment later, he heard her shout his name. She was panicked. The door flew open, and the bright sun rolled in along with her quickly finding all corners of the room. She held a newspaper to him. Her face lined, stricken with fear. Eddie was on the front page of the Tampa Tribune, an artist's rendering, and it looked just like him. Blonde Mary Rose was there too, not in a drawing but in a photograph.

How could this have happened? Had The Colonel talked? Had he gone to the press? Was he using Eddie to negotiate for something he wanted from authorities? Why pay for Eddie's cab back to the motel? Why not just call the police, turn him in? The article mentioned they were believed to be in Florida. The Colonel had to have been the source. Was he simply limiting the time Eddie had to think anything through? If that was the purpose, he was successful.

"We're in trouble, Eddie. They got us. What are we going to do?"

"Give me a minute."

He closed the curtains, paced. The Colonel wanted the money. If he cared more about gaining favor with law enforcement, Eddie and Mary Rose would already be in custody. He was leveraging Eddie to go through with the deal.

"We need to take the money somewhere else," Eddie finally said.

"Why?"

"Mary Rose, do you trust me?"

"With what? What do you mean?"

"We hide the money. If the police catch us afterwards, we tell them only I know where the money is. We tell them I forced you to come with me. You know nothing. The police will let you go, and at some point you pick the money up from wherever we leave it."

"Eddie, I don't want to go to Cuba by myself."

"It's my intention to come with you, but we have to be very careful."

"I trust you."

"Let's get everything together."

"What about the photographs in the newspaper?"

"No one at the motel has seen me. I came in last night in the middle of the night; same the night before when we checked in, and you were the one who registered us. They've only seen you with black hair. Basically, we stick to the plan. We just hide the money before we go back to The Colonel."

***

"You're late."

Eddie picked up on the agitation. His tardiness most likely triggered little concern. It was twenty minutes past two-thirty, the appointed time. A photographer was to arrive at three. Ten minutes remained. What frustrated The Colonel, Eddie supposed, was the obvious absence of the money. They held no bag or carrying case. Mary Rose held a small purse, too small for forty-seven thousand dollars. Behind thick glasses, The Colonel's eyes combed over the two of them. He stood behind his desk with opened blinds at his back, a cigarette burning in a tray.

"This is Mary Rose," Eddie said.

Twitches around his mouth and eyes let slip his lascivious appreciation. "Where's the money?" he asked. Though his eyes hadn't let go of Mary Rose, the question was for Eddie.

"It's close."

"I'm here to provide what I promised and you fail me?" The tone was fierce. The eyes moved off Mary Rose's figure and straight at Eddie.

Nervous, intimidated, Eddie shrugged. "Somehow our pictures landed in the afternoon papers. We need you. I wanted to make sure you needed us."

"You imagine I need your money?"

"You're taking some risk to get it."

"You think I was the one who tipped off the newspapers?"

A knock hammered the door. A tall, broad-shouldered man entered, insecure, eyes mostly to the floor. "Mr. Blackburn," he mumbled. "You asked for me at three." The man carried a Brownie Hawkeye camera with flash attachment.

"I appreciate you being punctual," The Colonel, apparently also known as Mr. Blackburn, said to him, "Bring the tool I mentioned?"

Without words, the man pulled hair clippers from a jacket pocket.

"Good."

"You want I should take the pictures here?" the lumbering man asked, still holding the clippers up.

After a nod, The Colonel said to Eddie, "I saw the Tribune. I asked this gentleman to cut your hair before taking your photograph. It should allow for an easier time with anyone who gets curious."

Not far back, Gene Green had been telling Eddie how smoothly everything would go at the Security Pacific. They weren't greedy; they wouldn't take all the money; they'd leave Mary Rose out of it. Don't worry about it, he said. You're making a mistake with the front door that probably won't even get noticed, he said.

"Thank you," Eddie muttered to The Colonel.

Everything moved quickly. After taking two or three inches from Eddie's hair and snapping photos, the tall man left. The Colonel carried on abetting the fugitives by ordering Cuban food as they waited on the identification cards. Knowing they'd no longer need it, Eddie offered the

Deluxe to The Colonel, and The Colonel responded as if he'd already planned to take it. "We'll have eyeballs looking out for you in Miami. They'll look for the Louisiana plates. Leave the door unlocked, keys in the glove box," he said before filling his mouth with something he called Masitas de Puerco.

They sat at a long table in another office, lots of food on paper plates, too much for the three of them. There were bottles of beer, candles lit. Eddie avoided the beer, wanting to keep his head straight. Mary Rose nibbled on a few things, mostly kept quiet. Eddie noticed her demeanor changed when she met The Colonel. Her voice returned to a more feminine, always-surprised sounding voice. She revealed few thoughts in her head, instead seemed to let her beauty communicate all she wished anyone to know.

The Colonel again brought up the subject of marriage and family. "It too can be a great motivator for getting out of poverty," he said.

Eddie wanted to tell him that murder and racketeering and selling drugs could get a man out of poverty too but instead said, "You have an interesting way of looking on the bright side."

"We're not going to be poor," Mary Rose responded, sounding suspicious.

The Colonel identified her suspicious tone, narrowed his eyes, and shifted his gaze to Eddie. Was he now thinking Eddie lied about the nearly fifty thousand dollars, that Mary Rose had just inadvertently revealed much larger rewards from the heist in Barstow? Eddie had assumed The Colonel knew the amount had been forty-eight grand before confronting him with questions. What if he didn't know?

Pressing again, clearly concerned, Mary Rose asked in a small voice, "Why would we be poor?"

Eddie should've told Mary Rose. He'd taken an insane chance. When they hid the money, Eddie told her they'd return for it on the way to the airport. He again told her to trust him.

The Colonel waved an ominously casual hand. His tone remained calm. "I don't like this feeling," he said. "Information I have asked for has not been truthfully provided. I really don't want to get upset."

Eddie leaned in, anxious, faltering without breath. "How do you say what you say about family and grandchildren and all that, and yet you take everything away, leave us with nothing?"

"You stole once, steal again," The Colonel snapped.

Mary Rose asked, "What's going on? What are we talking about?"

"He's taking all the money," Eddie admitted.

"You think my freedom doesn't cost me money?" The Colonel went on, bristling. He slammed a fist on the table, and then pointed a finger at Eddie, saying, "I give you a new start."

"I'm sorry," Eddie said. Mary Rose's face hung open, surprised. What was she thinking? What would she do? Eddie felt like he'd betrayed her.

The Colonel pushed his plate forward. "What stops you from getting on the plane without giving me the money, assuming the forty-seven thousand dollars is in fact the true amount?"

"It's the true amount," Eddie replied slowly. "And as far as you getting your money goes, I assume that if you don't, things could go bad for us. If we land in Havana and you don't have your money, I'd imagine there could be some guys waiting for us. I don't think these guys would make life pleasant for us on the island."

The Colonel put his face forward until candlelight reflected in his thick glasses. He spoke softly, and with the confidence of one who had the world in his palm. "We own that island. If you get off the plane and I don't have what I want, you'll be dead before your first cocktail." Turning to Mary Rose, he added, "Such a waste it would be."

"You'll get what you want, and you'll have our gratitude as well."

"Hand it to me now," The Colonel said roughly. "Why not get it over with?"

Eddie thought for a hard moment, and then shook his head. "Helping the police could buy you influence with them. If we give you the money, you can hide it just as easily as we can; tell the police we buried it in Texas or anywhere; you have no idea where it is. I won't give you the money and us at the same time. We'd be left with nothing. I'm sure you can understand. Give me a telephone number. I'll call as soon as we land. I'll tell you where the money is."

***

The five-hour drive from Tampa to Miami passed mostly in silence. Flight reservations were set for seven the next morning. Eddie had asked Mary Rose if she wanted to drive. She said, "No." Was she angry? For the millionth time, he tried thinking of an alternative way out of this mess, some last-minute possibility, a safe passage they had yet to consider. Leaving the country and never coming back was unfathomable, and yet they were about to make the jump. Silence from Mary Rose tore into his heart. He should never have deceived her. They needed each other. Didn't he know that?

Identification cards for each came out shockingly credible given the speed at which they were produced. Eddie's new name was Martin Thorne and he lived on the six hundred block of Alton Way in Tampa. Mary Rose became Lillian Robinson from San Diego. Eddie told her they would split up at the airport. They'd act like they didn't know each other. He'd drive into the parking lot, drop her off, and then drive around the block a couple of times before returning. He'd go into Miami International alone. If anyone asked about her, she would explain that a friend offered her a job at one of the casinos.

All his careful consideration was responded to as if he'd said nothing. He then explained extradition, emphasizing the need for a low profile should they make it to Cuba; the president there and the U.S. have a friendly relationship even though the president is in the pocket of known criminals like Meyer Lansky. From this point forward, Eddie had explained, they should never refer to each other by their old names, never mention Barstow. People like Connie Ackerman and Gene Green never existed and should never come up in conversation. "The past is all in your imagination now. It never happened," he said. "Let it go."

Her continued silence told him she wouldn't talk until he dealt with what she clearly perceived as a betrayal. Impatient with her unwillingness to understand and trust him at this crucial moment, Eddie became defensive. "If you had stayed away on the night of the heist you wouldn't be running from the law with me. You'd be free to do as you please. I didn't want you there. I was trying to protect you. I told Gene Green that was part of the deal, that you shouldn't be involved. You might've faced some awkward questions but you wouldn't have been a participant. You'd be all clear. That's what I asked for. That's what I wanted."

"He made me go. He didn't trust me."

She was hurt, comparing, Eddie felt sure, Gene Green's lack of trust to Eddie not revealing details about the money. "You're upset about the money, right? I should've told you," Eddie replied. "I'm truly sorry. Please understand that I was only trying to get us through this. That man we had dinner with was not going to negotiate. I was the one who was there with him. I didn't think you'd see it so clearly because you weren't with him like I was. There was no time to figure anything else out. These are dangerous people. The only way to work with them is to get in and out fast."

"It's fine."

Eddie thought he saw her clenched jaw soften. He wasn't sure. The night was starless, darkness had taken everything, and yet they continued on, barreling down the throat of a thick black sky, sometimes wondering if they were really going anywhere. The relentless gloom seemed to be without end. Quiet resumed, and time passed thoughtfully. Eventually, sixty miles northwest of Miami, with four hours remaining before their flight, they pulled into the parking lot of a diner. Arriving at the airport too early invited risk, Eddie knew. In addition, he needed rest. He was exhausted, and wanted to be fast thinking and watchful on his toes in the morning.

The diner was closed, all lights off. Hardly visible at the back of the diner, out of reach from passing headlights, Mary Rose complimented him, faintly in the quiet, affectionately. "You did good, Eddie."

"You're not upset?"

"You should've told me."

"You're right. It won't happen again."

"I can help make decisions too, you know."

"I know … I just … the hurdles are so huge, and they're one after the next. I hate putting such a burden on your shoulders."

"I can take it. Tell me what else is bothering you."

"What're we going to do about money?"

"I have a little. We'll be okay."

Surprised, Eddie squirmed. He danced fingertips over the steering wheel.

"What else?" she asked.

"I don't know."

"C'mon, tell me."

"Nothing can be done."

"What?"

"What that guy said about family and stuff ..."

"What about it?"

"It bothered me."

"Why?"

"Maybe it was true. How depressing to hear it from a guy who takes baseball bats to knees for a living."

"We have each other. We'll get through this together, Eddie," Mary Rose said, and she couldn't have sounded more sincere.

***

The swarm of bodies rattled his nerves. It was no different from a train station, Eddie thought, calming himself, having never been to an airport. He spotted Mary Rose. The time was six-forty. It occurred to him that the one piece of luggage she carried might not be believable for someone moving to Cuba. Wouldn't she have more?

Friendly staff in sharp suits greeted him. Before approaching the counter, he'd been asked three times if he needed assistance. They were annoyingly congenial. Bright smiles remained bright, giving no indication of recognizing him from newspapers.

He handed over a suitcase, told the nice-looking attendant his name was Martin Thorne. "Marty" he said right after, cloaking himself with as much casual innocence as possible.

"Brand new suitcase?" she asked.

Feeling a pinch of adrenaline, Eddie answered, "It is, in fact."

A ticket was offered without a request for identification, and he felt fairly lucky. Things moved smoothly. Escape seemed possible despite the extraordinary odds against them, until a loud male voice, amplified over an intercom, announced a delay. When the voice stopped, Eddie saw Mary Rose watching him from across the terminal. Her exquisite face held the alarmed expression he felt deep in his gut.

He was now falling or so it seemed. He sucked in air but couldn't regain his breath. What was the purpose behind the delay? How long would it last? Exposed among the crowd, his picture in the newspapers, nerves hit him worse than ever. His face went from shoulder to shoulder, imagining security forces or police officers marching his way. Why don't they just get it over with? Why torture him? His chest caved, crushing his heart.

When minutes passed and no one came, he grabbed a brochure from a rack, and sat with it unfolded to his face. He tried to find Mary Rose in his periphery but she had slipped away, vanished in the crowd.

All he could do was wait, and so he waited. What could anyone do? He had identification with his picture on it. It was in his wallet. He was Martin Thorne. He'd never heard of Eddie Howard. A fugitive? That sounded ghastly, he'd say, pretending to be someone different.

The crowd closed in around him, passengers with tickets for the same flight, waiting as well, becoming restless as the time stretched to seven-fifteen. Eddie still couldn't find Mary Rose. He closed his eyes and tried imagining himself anywhere else.

The voice returned, speaking over the intercom, apologizing for the delay, and announcing that boarding for Havana would commence. Eddie stood. Thankfully, he saw the back of Mary Rose. She stood at the front of the crowd. A door opened to the outside, and passengers began through it.

A flight attendant handed pre-paid postcards to every passenger. "What's it for?" Eddie inquired, and was told to, "Please write to a family member, mention you're enjoying a Pan Am flight to Havana, drop it in a mailbox when you land, your family member will be thrilled."

The airplane was impressive, its long silver body emblazoned by the morning sun. A stairway on wheels elevated passengers to the door at the side of the airplane, and when Eddie stepped from the terminal, Mary Rose was already making her way inside. She looked back at him briefly, carried a vulnerable expression, as a frightened child would to a parent. Eddie also felt apprehensive, lost and unsure considering the completely unknown path ahead. In addition to worries about their ultimate fate, though the airplane's beauty inspired confidence, Eddie remained concerned about the tremendous height they would reach, especially over the ocean.

Inside, the airplane was crowded by the time Eddie entered. His seat was next to Mary Rose. They continued to act as strangers. Each did a poor job masking nerves. Other passengers, however, smiling, making fast-friends, were apparently delighted by the adventure, convinced nothing could possibly go wrong.

It all happened quickly, almost too quickly. Engines rumbled and whined, wheels began to roll. Eddie wanted to go, needed his freedom, still felt entitled to it, and felt a rush from their capture so barely avoided but he also wished he could slam the brakes on the whole enterprise, not fly anywhere, race back to where he was known and beg forgiveness. Soon, though, they were charging down a runway. The velocity shoved Eddie deeper into his seat. He looked at Mary Rose and saw her eyelids pressed tightly shut. When they suddenly swooped into the air, it was such a startling and unnatural sensation that Eddie nearly cried out in horror. Up they climbed, higher and higher, and just as Eddie began to fear they'd gone too high, that the airplane might break apart, they leveled off, and Eddie noticed no alarm in the faces around him. He mimicked everyone else's unruffled composure, told himself to breathe easily, that he had only an hour to go.

Drinks came. Eddie and Mary Rose had coffee. Eddie finished his quickly. The mood of others remained jovial, as if waiting for a party. Eddie thought they all looked wealthy. Most were men, some appearing untrustworthy, perhaps even sordid. It was in their eyes, a ribald sparkle. Havana had been sold to the world as a dazzling all-night parade of fabulous showgirls and burlesque dancers. Such promises were completely foreign to Eddie, yet he wasn't without curiosity.

He pondered the ease of their navigation through Miami International and imagined The Colonel as possibly responsible. Perhaps he'd called in some favors with local law enforcement. Everyone had heard about police corruption linked to the mob.

Abruptly, the airplane dipped to one side, as if pulled by a giant invisible hand. Swells of panic were audible. Drinks spilled, including Mary Rose's coffee. A second dramatic tug pulled on the airplane. Eddie noticed the other passengers trying to remain good-humored. The pilot's voice came over the intercom. Without panic, he explained it was turbulence, apologized, said they should be through it before long, and to please remain seated.

Mary Rose turned to Eddie, and he'd never seen her so frightened. They lurched again. It seemed the airplane was out of control. The pilot returned, educating the passengers, saying air moves in streams, not unlike rivers against riverbanks, shifts in speed cause turbulence, altitude can shift ten or twenty feet, that's the jolt, there is no reason for alarm.

Despite reassurances, turbulence went on for another fifteen agonizing minutes. Far below, only ocean was visible. Eddie felt dizzy and unsteady even in his seat as he contemplated the empty miles and endless water below. His first experience told him enough; he hated flying. He closed his eyes and prayed for survival. He imagined lounging on a beach with beautiful Mary Rose at his side, smiles filled with secrets passed between them. Many happy years lived easily and without expectation. The worst was behind them, Eddie told himself repeatedly. They just needed to put tires to the Cuban ground.

When several minutes passed without difficulty, the flight attendant collected glasses and cups. She passed around napkins, apologized for the amusement park thrills. Mary Rose pointed at the coffee splatters on her dress, and the woman invited her to the rear of the airplane where she could dab at the dark splotches with a damp cloth. "Oh, well, I don't know," Mary Rose said, sounding feeble.

"We're through the turbulence, ma'am. You'll be just fine."

"Oh, well, okay."

Without her next to him, Eddie rubbed fingers into his forehead and took several long breaths. He then noticed Mary Rose left her purse. It was open. Pressed snugly within was the eight hundred dollars she had taken to purchase the Ford Deluxe. Eddie recognized the money easily because it was in the form of sixteen fifty-dollar bills folded in half. How had it come to be that she was still in possession of it? How had she paid for the car? He remembered it had taken her a long while. Had she offered herself to the salesman for it? Eddie felt his gut sinking. He was the victim of some deception. There could be no other possibility. Had she stolen the car?

When she returned, he said nothing. What could he say? He smiled at her. It was a fast anguished smile, and then the pilot spoke, mentioning Havana up ahead.

Eddie looked through a window. They descended and flew over much land. It was green. Some of it looked like jungle. It was exciting to see it from above, yet Eddie remained nerve-racked and heartbroken, unsure about the coming days. They passed over oddly shaped bodies of water, like giant ink spills on paper, reflecting perfect blue skies. He saw the city, a sprawling marvel of human creation, which from here forward, January 1957 to the end of his days, would be the place where he'd carry on but never call home.

Chapter Eleven

The buildings of the esplanade were crafted by architects from 18th century Paris and Vienna. It stretched from the oldest part of the city to the Malecón, and offered a view of the Morro Castle in the seaside distance. It was by far the most beautiful place Eddie had ever seen.

He and Mary Rose strolled alongside colonnaded mansions, faces angled to the Caribbean sunset, watching as it resurfaced old world grandeur with orange, bright as fire. The Prado dated back two hundred years. It reminded Eddie of every foreign-set picture he ever loved. He felt different in Havana. A weight had lifted. Everything seemed new, remarkably unrelated in any way to anywhere he'd been.

For three weeks Eddie and Mary Rose shared an apartment inside a long line of colonial houses with arches and balconies, a short walk from the Capitol building, El Capitolio, modeled after the Capitol building in Washington D.C., and where each evening's march along the Prado began. Eddie still had Life Magazine and Sears and Gene Kelly movies, but the new culture appealed to him immeasurably. He sipped strong dark coffee at an outside cafe in the mornings while watching Cuban people and wealthy internationalists as their days started. A man in a straw boater and linen suit played Spanish guitar. Young children sold bananas. Cigar and saltwater scented breezes ruffled the trees.

Dance halls and casinos pushed the city's energy into the night so days were calm, allowing a handful of hours for recovery, followed by a walk in the cooling sun before the city came to life again. Eddie and Mary Rose hadn't involved themselves much with the city's popular attractions. They were getting settled, looking for jobs.

Eddie had prescription glasses again and marveled at what he'd been missing.

He tried for a job as bookkeeper at a casino called San Souci. His interview was before noon, so he saw nothing of the floorshow advertised as an authentic voodoo ritual performed by scantily clad dancers backed by ferocious jungle rhythms. He talked about his experience keeping ledgers and even mentioned ERMA as potentially advantageous to the gaming industry in coming years, but for some reason wasn't hired.

He responded to an ad for a dishwasher at the Sevilla-Biltmore, the most luxurious hotel among so many. Like a palace or cathedral, ten stories high with rooftop ballroom and extraordinary view of the city and the sea, Eddie felt special just looking at it. The design had an oriental or Arabic flare, Eddie couldn't tell, but he thought washing dishes in such a place would be a fine thing to do. He was to follow up with the manager in the morning, hoping they'd give him at least a few hours per week.

Mary Rose decided to revisit her earlier ambition of wanting to sell women's fashions. A small hat store along the Prado needed help. They hired someone shortly before Mary Rose became aware of the position, but asked for a way to contact her should anything change, and Mary Rose soon heard from them. They liked her a great deal. Eddie thought they must recognize the advantage an attractive young American woman could bring to their establishment. They told her a pregnant employee would be leaving in four months, and they'd save that vacant position just for her. This made Mary Rose very happy. It was a stepping-stone toward the future she always wanted.

In three weeks, Eddie hadn't seen a single pair of suspicious eyes. There was no reason to anticipate problems from the criminal element in the city. As promised, Eddie called The Colonel upon landing, told him Mary Rose and he had stopped at a bicycle store the night they came by. At the location where The Colonel's subordinate took Eddie's wallet, stood an old bicycle with decayed tires. Eddie and Mary Rose replaced the old tires with new ones. Within the new tires was the entire forty-seven grand. In some ways, Eddie was glad to be rid of it.

New identities proved to be unproblematic as well. Potential employers were told Eddie met a young woman, they were looking for adventure someplace far from everything they'd ever known, and then Eddie would snicker, and say, "If I tell you too much about Marty Thorne's life in Cleveland you'll fall asleep." Everyone in Havana seemed to like that.

Passing a pair of elegant women in high heels and sleeveless tops, Mary Rose said, "I love it here so much," as a cool wind welcomed them to the Malecón, the wide roadway along the waterfront. The sun's final rays reflected off open faces of buildings stretching far in each direction. The light lingered in the ocean spray, glowing, filling the air with gold, and transforming the island's northern edge with a majestic radiant luster.

Chrome fenders and windshields on cars also brightened with the fire-orange of the falling sun. Waves crashed higher with the late tide. Some water leapt high enough to fall into the road and form puddles that quickly seeped into cracks and crevices, before presumably slipping back into the sea. Eddie pondered the water as it repeatedly and relentlessly crashed against the wall. As he did so, questions he wanted to ask Mary Rose for the last couple of weeks returned. "Do you think about things … you know, what happened before? All of this. Do you think about it much?"

"No. Should I?"

"I don't know. I guess you shouldn't. I was just wondering."

"Do you?" she asked.

"Yeah. I can't stop thinking about it. I wish I could stop. I wish I could be like you and just ... let it go. I like it here. But I can't stop thinking about ... everything that happened before."

What had his sister been thinking? What about Lynette and Sue? Eddie imagined he remained a popular topic of conversation. Maybe he'd done Barstow a favor, confirmed suspicions of him, and provided those who knew him with reason to feel superior.

Mary Rose slipped her fingers between his, held his hand, and said, "Let it go, Eddie. Just let it go."

***

When Eddie went back to the Sevilla-Biltmore the next morning, he was offered the dishwasher job. The pay, though small, felt significant. Soon after, a soft-spoken kitchen manager named Ernesto Castellanos trained him. Mr. Castellanos spoke English, nevertheless, he patiently taught Eddie words like *un cuchillo* for knife and *un tenedor* for fork because most of the kitchen staff's English was limited, and he explained that good communication was essential for things to run smoothly. The work was unlike any Eddie had ever done and he found it, in addition to the foreign environment, more than a little intimidating.

When left to do the job on his own, Eddie feverishly focused on trying to recall all of Mr. Castellanos' instructions regarding the various responsibilities. He had to mop the floor, empty and fill the water tubs, make sure they had sanitizing solution in them, change the dishwater in the dish machine hourly, take garbage to a dumpster, and only use the freight elevator when doing so, sort and rinse dirty dishes and place them in racks to send through the dish machine, and carry clean dishes to the cook's line. Some things needed washing manually like pots, pans, and trays. He had to notify Mr. Castellanos when the dish machine or rinse cycle fell below certain temperatures. It was also his responsibility to keep restrooms clean.

As to the other employees, Eddie had a natural resistance to initiating friendships. He felt, even long before becoming Marty Thorne, new friendships required a false presentation of him, and therefore he typically avoided the effort. With the kitchen staff at the Sevilla-Biltmore, however, the choice wasn't his to make. It took a few shifts but the other fellows soon came around to welcoming him as one of their own, helping him whenever he needed it.

Eddie rapidly grew to enjoy the people he worked with, the camaraderie being unlike anything he'd ever experienced. He imagined introducing them to Mary Rose, maybe inviting one or two to the apartment. Feelings for Mary Rose were beyond friendship, and so the possibility of a Cuban kitchen worker as a pal, someone nice who could further acclimatize them to the island, was enormously appealing.

One young co-worker, a fellow who spoke with difficult English, named Lolo Hornedo, was practicing hard after hours to become a drummer. In the kitchen, he drummed on pots and pans, counters, anything in front of him, using ladles and spoons and whisks. Lolo told Eddie that Mr. Castellanos didn't like him, that one day he said something about Mr. Castellano's beautiful wife and Mr. Castellanos overheard it, and took it the wrong way. Consequently, Lolo worried about losing his job in the kitchen. He needed the money if he was to move to Europe or America and play with the big bands. Lolo told Eddie that one of the two older dishwashers, Ricardo Sotolongo, was secretly telling Mr. Castellanos that Lolo was still saying things about his wife behind his back, and Ricardo Sotolongo did this because Lolo once complained about him standing around too much, letting dishes stack up, and taking the trash out and not coming back for twenty minutes. Eddie told him he would find an opportunity to tell Mr. Castellanos how impressive Lolo was, and that he'd not seen anyone work harder, and that put a big smile on the young man's face.

Alian Aldama's dishwashing money supported his mother who opened a cafe. She could cook the best dishes in Havana, shredded beef with onions and criolla sauce, beef stuffed with carrot and chorizo sausage, "better than this hotel food," Alian said quietly, but his mother's cafe was small and looked like a licensing office, so the whole family was pitching in to give the place some life. When Eddie told Alian what Lolo said about Ricardo, Alian said Ricardo's cousin is a manager at the company that provides the sanitizing solution for the kitchen. It comes at a great discount because of this relationship, and that is why Ricardo takes liberties and doesn't work as hard as others.

The fastest friend Eddie made was Alejandro Fuentes. The others in the kitchen teased Alejandro constantly. He was a skinny, quiet Cuban teen. He was the type who could take the teasing well. Great big blocks of white teeth in Alejandro's mouth would flare anytime someone made a joke about him. They handed him trays filled with dirty dishes and asked him to carry the cumbersome racks into the dining room. They would do this, not because he was so skinny, but because months earlier an elegant and beautiful woman entered as guest, and Alejandro felt an uncontainable desire to get an up-close look at her. He grabbed a tray of dirty dishes and marched through the dining room, pretending to have some purpose, and when he returned, Mr. Castellanos gave him a vicious scolding, as the racks were never permitted to cross the dining room floor. It was a story told over and over and always with much laughter.

Eddie's enthusiasm for this new relationship grew when he heard Alejandro referencing scenes from American movies. For the first time in years, Eddie was able to talk to someone who loved movies and had seen almost all the recent ones. During a break, they stood in the alley next to the dumpster, and Eddie mentioned how *King of the Khyber Rifles* made him feel right there, how exciting it was, how all the details seemed so real, and that after he saw it, he spent weeks wishing he could ride a horse. "Have you ever been on a horse, Alejandro?"

The Bribe was another they each saw. Ava Gardner's turn to the camera when she first appeared in the picture was breathtaking. Alejandro made the point that it was impossible to imagine that Charles Laughton knew there was a camera near him because he was so convincing. The teenage Cuban called *Viva Zapata!* the greatest picture of all, better than anything ever made. Eddie saw the Marlon Brando picture and liked it, but didn't think it compared with some others. The Robert Mitchum movie *Macao* reminded Eddie of *The General Died at Dawn*, which went back too far for Alejandro to have seen, but the films offered a similar escape, Eddie told him, and he wished Alejandro could've seen it. When Alejandro commented on *The Prowler,* Eddie said he thought Van Heflin was great, and that he watched *South of Algiers* four times in one week.

Eddie mentioned to Alejandro that Lolo worries about losing his job because of Ricardo, and Alejandro told Eddie that Lolo wants to make love to Mr. Castellanos' wife, talks about it all the time, and should learn when to open his mouth and when not to. Alejandro also told Eddie that he liked Mr. Castellanos, Mr. Castellanos was right about the dishes, but Mr. Castellanos also insists they work on the holiday celebrating independence, and that is wrong. Eddie couldn't understand how that would be possible in the hotel business, but he said nothing, as Alejandro seemed very worked up about it.

Sleep was easier for Eddie as the hours filling his days chiseled into routine. It all happened so fast. What happened to Gene Green? The safe technician obviously shot him. Would he ever find out why? How many big questions go unanswered? It was a problem, Eddie felt, and he wished he could solve it, yet he'd exhausted his brain ruminating on loose ends, and couldn't keep demanding answers where there were none.

Mary Rose remained in many ways the woman she had been, her high heels planted firmly in the present day. Was it her youth that waved away any reflective moods? Restless during her days without work, she explored. American magazines advertising the latest fashions accompanied her, and if she grew very bored with the streets around her apartment, she'd hop into a taxi and put her eyes to the further reaches of the city. Eddie told her he didn't like her venturing out too much, that he'd heard things about violence from groups upset with the government.

"You should see the swimming pools inside these exquisite hotels, and all kinds of interesting people drinking cocktails in the middle of the day. Oh, and then I went to a street called Zanja, and saw what must surely have been prostitutes out in the street. They'd appear in doorways, and then disappear. It was all so shockingly out in the open. Oh, and did you know the presidential palace is just a few blocks from where you work? Oh, and guess what? You're going to be so excited. That actor you were interested in, George Raft, I found out which casino he's always in. It's called the Casino de Capri."

Would Eddie ever ask about the eight hundred dollars? How would they have survived their first month in Cuba without it? From a certain point of view, Eddie had been living off her generosity. In addition, as he thought about it, he was afraid of knowing too much about her. She remained as much a puzzle to him as ever, and he worried that if he found some way to put all the pieces together, so he could see her clearly, she might run away.

For now, he put his thinking into the future, tried continuously to let go of the past, recognizing that his new life would never be anything like his old life. There was much excitement. Once they could afford new clothes and a few costly drinks, they could go see George Raft. Havana was a place of unending mystery. Anything could happen and far too much had already happened. The island had a deep and tragic and fascinating history.

As well, the Cuban people were different. Observations Eddie and Mary Rose made, favorably comparing Cubans to Americans, in the initial weeks of their new lives, eventually became nuanced. Differences took on complexity with time. Similarities, not so visible at first, surfaced, and yet the people remained surprising. Reflecting on nearly fifty years in Barstow, Eddie wondered what it was all for. Was it just time, filled up and thrown out? In Cuba, everything was different. Everything was moving. The city had a life to it, and it was impossible to imagine it could ever stop.

Chapter Twelve

"It tortures me to be near her."

"And it is worse to be away." Alejandro's white smile flashed as he said this.

"I wish she'd give me a sign," Eddie admitted. "Or tell me she might give me a sign someday."

As the first month of the year rolled into the second, Eddie's friendship with Alejandro flourished. They spent time together some mornings before the restaurant opened. He thought back to The Colonel's words about having children given his slightly paternal feeling for his young friend.

Alejandro also assumed the role of Eddie's confidant, a sympathetic listener to his misery. The pain Eddie referred to over and over had to do with his intense affection for Mary Rose. They shared food and drinks, collaborated on furniture and decorations for the apartment. They seemed to appreciate each other, yet she found no bridge to cross in becoming more than friends.

The young Cuban had never been in love, Eddie knew, but he did know something about it from films, as he mentioned many times, "The love got him very bad," referring to film stars like Montgomery Clift in pictures like *A Place in the Sun*.

This morning, as with so many mornings, Eddie and Alejandro strolled past a coffee stand, a shoeshine man, pamphleteers, seagulls relaxing in the air, and the smells of breakfasts sizzling inside small cafes.

"She's young like you," Eddie said. "I understand where someone might feel they have their whole life to live and don't want to get married so quickly, but we have so much in common, especially now that we're here. The other Americans are only here temporarily."

"How you see her only with American?"

"There would be nothing wrong with her being with a Cuban fellow but, as I say, we have things in common. We both know America. It's where we come from. It's our foundation."

"You say the two of you seek adventure, different, everything different."

"You think it's a bad thing we have stuff in common? You're saying she might want to find a man here because he's from here, he's different?"

"Why not?"

Eddie scratched his head. "I don't know. I hadn't thought about that."

"Buy flowers."

"I think she knows I like her. I'm afraid if I make some obviously overt gesture, something romantic, it could backfire. I don't want her to feel funny around me. She could start avoiding me because it's awkward, and then I'd have even less of her than I have now."

"Perhaps you should become a dancer," Alejandro suggested, not without a little humor.

Eddie shook his head dismissively, and changed the subject. "Say, I heard something yesterday. Ricardo told me that twenty-five or thirty years ago, Al Capone stayed in room six-fifteen at the Sevilla-Biltmore. He'd rented the whole sixth floor for his pals."

"I have heard," Alejandro nodded, looking off. "Yes."

"That's amazing."

Alejandro jammed hands in his pants-pockets and said nothing for a while. He seemed suddenly annoyed, and Eddie was aware enough of the mood change to keep quiet as well, though he didn't know what bothered his friend. In the distance was the colossal Hotel Nacional, its twin spires pricking blue skies.

Finally, Alejandro turned back to him. "Eddie, we are close," he said with a seriousness that conflicted with his youthful buoyancy. It was a seriousness Eddie was unaccustomed to from his friend.

"Sure, we are."

The young Cuban moved near and spoke softly. "Your Mary Rose, she goes walking. She walks and walks during the day. Tell her no Calle twenty-three today. In Vedado. Not today."

"What?"

"I am your friend. Say nothing. Except your woman. Tell her."

"I don't understand. Alejandro, what does this mean?"

"Just that I have heard things." The young Cuban put a finger to his lips, again demanding secrecy. "I go. Maybe see you later today," he said before rushing off, leaving Eddie alone and confused.

Eddie was sure he must've offended Alejandro in some way. They had been having a nice conversation, and it was a conversation they'd had several times before. For a moment, he thought maybe he'd talked of Mary Rose too much, and then he wondered what it meant to avoid Calle twenty-three. It was a major thoroughfare. Which part? What had Alejandro heard? Eddie struggled for answers throughout the remainder of the morning. Cubans carried within them strange beliefs brought from Africa and passed through generations. They were superstitious and unwavering believers in pagan rituals. Curses were summoned and supported by claims of closeness with Changó. Eddie had seen buckets of clean water dumped in streets to ward off evil spirits. He'd heard of bloodied feathers placed at doorsteps. Had Alejandro's warning been something to do with this? Had their past caught up to them in some way?

At work, hours later, a faulty steam inlet valve brought commotion to the kitchen. In the middle of a hectic lunch every glass, plate, and utensil had to be washed manually. Even Mr. Castellanos rolled up his sleeves, and sank his hands into the frenzy of rinsing, soaping and scrubbing. Like young soldiers on kitchen patrol, they gave the task everything, and carried it off with humor. A bowl flew from Eddie's slippery mitts and shattered. "No pay this week," Mr. Castellanos joked with Eddie, as they kept up the work. After twenty minutes, Alian had the valve fixed.

The young dishwasher who worked so hard for his mother's cafe took a few pats on the back after that, and things calmed to a normal pace. Mr. Castellanos said something in Spanish and got a laugh, and then the host from the dining room entered. He was a dapper man with a carefully groomed mustache, and sometimes the kitchen crew made jokes because he wore too much Chanel Pour Monsier. In this moment, he had a look of fear on his face Eddie had never seen on the man before. He spoke to Mr. Castellanos, and his words put a grim look on the kitchen manager's face. Eddie couldn't understand what was said, but knew it had to be something terrible because the whole staff stopped working. They stood quietly next to the hum of discharge lines, spray pipes, and tank drives.

"What is it?" Eddie asked.

Mr. Castellanos answered, "Machine guns."

For some moments, all held back words. Shock arranged the face of each differently. "Anyone hurt?" Eddie asked at last.

"They won't say. Probably so."

"Who was it?"

"Don't know."

"Where?"

"Calle twenty-three."

Eddie's first thought was to run and find Mary Rose, however, he quickly realized he'd look suspicious. Even now, they unquestionably thought it odd that an American, at nearly fifty, would move to Cuba to wash dishes. A sudden exit, on the heels of street violence would invite further scrutiny. What could he do?

He'd said nothing to Mary Rose about Alejandro's warning. It seemed such a strange occurrence, too strange to pass off to someone else. Would she have heeded the warning if he'd mentioned it? There were no specifics.

Eddie's schedule for the day was the opposite of Alejandro's. He was to end at three, while Alejandro would start at four. Would Alejandro show up? Eddie wondered how he would manage the next two and a half hours knowing nothing. He tried consoling himself with the probability Mary Rose was nowhere near Calle twenty-three at the time of the shooting. What was Alejandro's involvement? He knew something. What did he know? How had he come to know it? Could he have been a participant in such horror?

Several days earlier, Eddie had met Mr. and Mrs. Fuentes, Alejandro's parents. He had dinner at their home, and though they didn't speak English, their gentle natures were written on their faces, emanated from their bones. Two sisters, one older than Alejandro and one younger, each flashed the same goofy smile that made Alejandro so endearing. Eddie envied the warmth and closeness, the obvious affection. He believed nothing nefarious could possibly come from such a home.

Thoughts among kitchen staff remained unspoken. Mr. Castellanos turned a radio on to a low volume but Eddie couldn't understand what was said. Passing minutes crawled. Eddie felt anxiety sickening him. He wondered what kind of rage could cause someone to raise a machine gun. The wait seemed worse when the dining room became nearly vacant. News of the violence had spread quickly, and the staff had little to do. They stood solemnly listening to the radio or lost within their private thoughts. When finally Eddie raced home, he found the apartment empty.

Where was Mary Rose? Would she never return? What happened?

***

Sunlight dimmed on turquoise louver doors that led onto the balcony. Inside, Eddie didn't touch the lamps, preferring to sit in darkness. Worries about Mary Rose and Alejandro spread like a disease, blanketing his insides in darkness as well. He'd lost so much, he reflected, even his name. He cared for two people, and at times wondered if he even knew them. He stared at a cream-colored brick wall. A shadow from the balcony grill had been climbing the wall while fading. It had round, sweeping curves that surged and swelled like a row of odalisques.

The day had been the longest he'd experienced since leaving Miami. Excruciating anxiety that squeezed like an iron vice should be a thing of the past, he thought. Yet here it was all over again.

At long last, the doorknob jangled. Mary Rose entered, and Eddie felt some relief. As she lit the apartment she asked why he was sitting in darkness, wanted to know if he'd eaten, also said she had big news to tell him.

Still troubled, Eddie asked, "Where were you?"

"Oh, you wouldn't believe what I saw. Truly terrifying. Everything was quiet. I was walking down the street. Suddenly, I hear a rumble. You want a Mojito? I'm going to make myself one. Other people on the street start looking around too. It gets louder and louder, this rumble, until suddenly before us, coming around a corner is a tank. Oh, Eddie, my gosh! It rumbled toward us, and then it was followed by another tank. Motorcycles from the military were zipping by, jeeps. Everyone had big guns, and they were moving so fast. I didn't realize tanks could—"

There was a knock on the door. Without questioning the caller, Mary Rose opened it. A Cuban, shy of forty, with soft brown eyes clearly familiar with Mary Rose, appeared. He stood broad-shouldered, handsome.

"Ramón."

Smiling, he handed her a Bazaar magazine with Audrey Hepburn on the cover. Eddie recognized it as something that had been in the apartment for days. "You left this in the car," he said.

"Oh," she replied. "How considerate. Would you like to come in?"

His smile widened and he waved at Eddie. "No. I go," he said, and left.

"Bye."

Eddie sat stunned as Mary Rose shut the door. She then went to the kitchen. His heart raced to deny what his eyes witnessed. He was a taxi driver, Eddie reasoned, or a man who gave her a lift after the tanks had terrorized her. Eddie stood, went out onto the balcony, and saw Ramón drive away in a yellow Buick Roadmaster convertible. He remained on the balcony for some time after it was gone.

"I wonder what was happening," he heard her call from deep within the apartment. Moments later, she was behind him. He could feel her at his back. He faced the city lights, unable to look at her.

"The tanks," she went on.

"There was a shooting," he said after a time.

"Oh, my."

"Who's your friend?"

"Ramón is just someone I met."

Without turning, Eddie said, "He looks like a film star, a Rudy Valentino."

"He's teaching me things."

Eddie whirled and marched inside, passing Mary Rose without a glance. He stopped near the front door and his head sunk into his shoulders. "He didn't come knocking on your door so he could return some stupid magazine."

"Eddie …" she said defensively, and his name was all he heard before he was gone.

***

Alejandro stumbled into the night. He hauled heavy trash-bags a short distance before he stopped, took a breath, and then heaved the bags off the ground a few feet further. Eddie moved from shadows, and helped his friend get the bags in place for the morning's truck. He'd been waiting, anxious to reveal his heartbreak about Mary Rose and get answers about his friend's connection to the day's violence. Alejandro had no smile for him. The Cuban teen looked at Eddie as if he'd have preferred to see anyone else.

"What's going on?" Eddie muttered.

"I should never have spoken."

"Alejandro, we're friends."

Alejandro nodded, and said, "I must return to the dishes."

"Tell me."

Alejandro's eyes peered into blackened distances, and then he stepped closer to Eddie, whispering. "We have one who leads this country who does not care, and for saying that I could be arrested and thrown in jail."

Eddie sighed, having heard his answer.

"People listen to our conversations," Alejandro went on, tightening his young face into a knot. "They listen everywhere. There is no safe place. Batista tells people that what he does, he does for them. Not true. Everything he does, he does to bring wealth to himself, more wealth than you imagine. We are slaves. There is nothing we can do but fight. The only way out is to fight. We have been fighting. Has he listened? No, because he is no longer one of us. He used to be. He comes from same background as all of us. If anyone should care about the Cuban people, it should be him but it is not. He has become a piece of fuzz found in the pockets of American companies. He's used, and he does not mind being used. There are many of us who are willing to be hurt. We fight for liberation. We fight for what is ours. We fight to stop someone from taking from us. How many *Habanos* do you see walking the streets with their head held high wearing nice clothes? We are a people who have become servants. He turns us into servants because he himself is a servant. He does not mind being a servant because he takes so much money. He lives like a king."

"Alejandro, it's unbelievably dangerous. It's crazy to be involved in something like this. So, your friends shoot some people, then what? Where do you go? What do you do?"

"Do you even listen?"

Eddie sounded like his sister, he knew, and he told himself to stop. What did he know about any of this? Absurdly, reaching out for a friendship he felt was running away, he said, "If something happens to you, think of the movies you'll miss."

"I fight for the children I hope to have one day," Alejandro replied, "that they may have opportunities denied to me."

Eddie's eyes fell within briefly, and then he shrugged, and said, "I don't know, Alejandro. I'm ignorant of so much, and this may be an area where I have little knowledge, but I do know Batista has the military on his side. Is there any way to combat that? If there is, tell me. What're you going to do?"

"I have to go," Alejandro said, before leaving Eddie alone.

For two hours, Eddie roamed. Night air dampened, and it was very late when streaming crowds thinned from plazas and corridors. To Eddie it seemed he couldn't hold onto anything. Ever since Mary Rose walked into the Security Pacific, his life had been in a constant state of reaching for something and finding nothing. As he rounded a corner, ambling between tall buildings, his apartment on the second floor of one, he saw again, now glistening beneath a high moon in the narrow path of sky, Ramón's yellow Buick Roadster.

How could Mary Rose do this? Had she rushed down the street to the pay phone when Eddie left and called him? Were they in love? Had she been too cowardly to step forward and break Eddie's heart with honesty? Eddie entered and found them seated across from one another, drinks and candles on the table. She took a long drag off a cigarette and blew a cloud into the high ceiling. Eddie had no idea how to react. His rage muted and crippled him.

Breaking a thick silence, Mary Rose finally spoke. "Eddie, what's wrong?"

"What's wrong? Nothing. Everything's terrific."

Recognizing the tightness in his voice, the anger, she pressed. "Eddie, why are you acting so crazy?"

"Acting like what? What do you mean?"

Ramón stood. "I go."

Locking eyes on the Cuban, Eddie said, "You'll be back later though, right? Maybe after I've gone to bed you can come by."

Ramón headed for the door, his face grimaced with pity for Eddie, who went straight for the balcony. Eddie heard Mary Rose and Ramón whispering at the door. Eddie felt stabbed by their whispers, ensnared and pierced from all sides.

With Ramón gone, Mary Rose approached Eddie, standing within the turquoise louver doors. Eddie could feel her behind him, exactly as they'd been hours earlier. "So, am I not allowed to get on with my life?" she asked.

Eddie said nothing. His brain felt like a block of stone, a dead thing that all the screaming from his heart could never resuscitate.

"You won't talk to me. Great."

"I couldn't stop you from getting on with your life if I wanted to. You're great at getting on with things."

"What does that mean?"

"Just that you move pretty fast from one person to the next."

An explosion punctured the night-covered city, probably fifteen blocks away. Shocked, Eddie and Mary Rose stood staring for a time. The orange glow of fire poured upward toward the stars. Sirens soon wailed.

"Revolution?"

"Yes," Eddie answered, as lights in apartment windows awakened and soon spread across the landscape. Attacks were said to be increasingly frequent no matter how brutal Batista's retaliation.

"Eddie, I'm sorry if I've hurt you in some way."

"If you've hurt me?" he snapped incredulously, and then pushed past her back into the apartment. "What's wrong with you that you can't ... don't you have any feelings at all? What if this man is part of the revolution? Do you even know this man?"

Following him, Mary Rose asked, "It seems like you felt like there was something between us but what was there?"

"Nothing."

"If there was something, if you felt something, why didn't you mention it?"

"Mary Rose, I'm here because of you."

"That's not true."

"It is true. It is painfully, pathetically true."

"You never said anything."

"Of course I did."

"Eddie, you never said anything. You're the quietest person I've ever met in my life. You don't talk about how you feel. You don't express anything."

"Words? Words would've made all the difference?"

"Yes. We're not cave-people, Eddie. Words matter. Communication matters. I knew you liked looking at me. I didn't know anything else."

"So if I'd expressed my true feelings for you, those feelings would've been returned? Is that what you're telling me?"

"I don't know."

"You don't know? How can you not know?"

"I'm being honest."

"Honestly, if you think Ramón will give you more than his eyes you're an idiot."

"There's no need to be cruel."

"What have you given me? Huh? What have you said to me? Nothing."

"I came with you, Eddie. I could've stayed with Gene."

"If you had you'd be dead alongside him right now but you probably knew that. You probably sensed the old safe technician was psychotic. You knew something bad was coming, and so you got out just in time."

"That's not true."

"Well, it had nothing to do with me, that's for sure."

"It did. I wanted to be with you."

"How'd you pay for the car in Louisiana?"

"What?"

"The car in Louisiana, the Ford Deluxe, how'd you pay for it?"

She hesitated, clearly surprised, and then said, "With money from the heist." She went to the table, blew out the candles, grabbed half-emptied glasses, and marched them into the kitchen. "This is ridiculous. You knew that. You knew I used the money from the bank. How else would I have paid for it? There's something wrong with you, Eddie."

"Answer the question."

"I did answer the question!" she shouted.

"There were sixteen fifty-dollar bills that you took to purchase a car. You came back with a car, and that same eight hundred dollars was in your purse afterwards."

With a clenched jaw, she washed the glasses, blinking rapidly, fighting tears.

"How'd you get the car?" Eddie went on. "Not talking now?"

"Stop it!" she cried, and Eddie heard his father's voice in hers.

Still, he couldn't back off. He was a dog on a bone, ferociously wearing her down. "I imagine you prostituted yourself for it. I also imagine it wasn't the first time you got something that way."

Mary Rose turned the faucet off and stood shaking, sobbing, staring into the sink. Eddie watched, suddenly wanting to console her from his vicious attack, but he did nothing, and then she said, "You're right, Eddie. I'm no good." She went into the bedroom after that, and didn't come out until after Eddie left in the morning.

***

The Big Combo with Richard Conte was playing at the Teatro Rodi on Linea Street in Vedado. Outside, Eddie watched as people with few cares on their faces lined up for the eight o'clock showing. The night was breezy, pushing papers in the street and ruffling clothes. Eddie imagined a great storm out at sea, violently churning yet too far away to keep people indoors.

Alejandro had come by the restaurant during lunch and asked Eddie to meet at the cinema in the evening. The request to meet pleased Eddie, not just because he cherished the friendship, and felt he needed the young Cuban in his life, but also because he didn't want to be at the apartment with Mary Rose. They hadn't spoken since four nights earlier, the night Ramón appeared twice and the revolution put black clouds over the city.

Amidst the conflux of filmgoers, Alejandro appeared, walking alongside a lean, dark middle-aged man. "My friend," Alejandro said, aiming a thumb at the man but not giving him a name.

"We walk and talk," Alejandro said. "My friend has many details."

They put their faces into the wind and walked toward the Malecón. "I'm not a part of this," Eddie said. "I'm not going to be a part of it. I've never been a soldier. I don't know why you're telling me anything."

"It is important to Alejandro that you understand what we are up against."

Eddie shrugged, mystified by the grave drama presented to him. "Okay."

Little else was said as they covered four or five blocks. For some reason, Eddie thought of his sister as they walked, and imagined it was not yet nighttime in California. They soon strolled along the wall until reaching a place where the waves came near, but not far enough to crash up onto the road. It was dark, and they stood among rocks. The blackened Caribbean fell loudly as it reached to swallow them up, and Alejandro's friend had to nearly shout his words.

"In the last few years American investments went from one hundred and fifty million dollars to nearly one billion dollars. In just the last few years," he emphasized. "Why? Because there is much money to be made. The people of Cuba have seen none of this money. All profits have gone into hands of corrupt politicians and American investors, many who do not work within the legal system of your own country. Having said this, it is not just the unlawful ones, but the lawful ones who plunder the riches of this island. American government pays financial support to the Cuban government in order to do nothing about enormous profits made by American corporations off the backs of Cuban workers. Three years ago, our president created Banco de Desarrotto Económico y Social. This is a decree by which he takes the people's money, promises it will be spent on public works projects, necessities. Instead, he hands the money to investors who want to build more hotels and casinos for tourists. In order for American interests to take advantage of these generous subsidies, they pay large initial kickback to the president, monthly operating fees to the president plus a percentage of profits to the president. Suddenly we have the Hilton, the Deauville, the Capri. Batista is said to be making millions while the people of Cuba remain poor. Rich businessmen, rich politicians, and rich gangsters trade money back and forth, get richer, and the people remain poor. When the outcry becomes too great, our current president promises social reforms, advancements in education, implying the Cuban people are too stupid to become wealthy when the truth is, he is not smarter than us, he is a thief. It is not intelligence that has granted him his reward. It is a black heart, corruption, thievery. However, tragically, he gets through to some people, this man who I cannot even bear to say his name, when the women are offered a chance to vote, how easily they forget their vote counts for nothing. Political rivals have their throats cut. If the press reports on the throat cutting, they also have their throats cut. Now, we have a revolution leader who knows the true crimes of the wealthy and privileged because he is the son of a landowner. He has had money and turned his back on it. He is one we can trust."

"Look," Eddie said, also raising his volume. "I don't doubt anything you're saying. I just don't know what it has to do with me. Why are you telling me any of this?"

"Alejandro should never have told you about Calle twenty-three. He is young. It was a mistake. It jeopardizes us, creates weakness. If you tell anyone about him, that person will be tortured until he or she speaks."

Eddie was surprised to find Alejandro crying. Eddie first thought it a reaction to Cuba's tragic circumstances, but as tears shed faster, and his young friend began to shake, Eddie wondered if the emotion was from something else.

"I'm not going to tell anyone," Eddie said. "Alejandro is my friend. I wouldn't do anything that could hurt him or anyone he cares for."

"That is good. Good to hear. Understand, we cannot fail. All who stand behind Castro understand that no cost is too great. Sacrifices will be difficult but necessary. People think Havana is all games. Roll dice, win prizes. Havana is life, Mr. Thorne, and life is no game."

"My name's not Thorne," Eddie admitted. "I robbed a bank in California," he went on, and then stopped, letting them imagine the rest.

The three let waves crash into their thoughts, and then finally the man nodded, and moved up the rocks to the wall and the city, gone forever. Eddie didn't know why he admitted this. He also didn't know why Alejandro was blubbering so uncontrollably. He did, however, know that his confession sprang from a survival instinct. He felt safer saying it. A moment later, Alejandro too climbed away from the sea, and Eddie was left to look out at nothing, questioning how fortunate he was to still be alive.

Chapter Thirteen

Sporting a linen suit by the Italian designer Brioni, and a Panama hat, Eddie stepped from the bedroom. He displayed himself for scrutiny while Mary Rose, who looked like a movie star, sat waiting, smoking, and wearing a floral print dress. Light from the balcony touched her softly and seemed incapable of moving past her into the apartment.

"You're not wearing your bowtie," she said.

"I just haven't put it on yet."

"Put it on. I wish to see."

The architecture in Havana became more impressive once Spring arrived. Tall ceilings lifted the intense heat upward. Substantial openings between rooms carried even the gentlest of breezes. In a corner, a large split-leaf philodendron, known for its ability to shrug off hurricanes, sat exhausted from the hot day, loopy and green and unmoving.

Eddie, on the other hand, felt light on his feet, more youthful than he'd felt in some time. Mary Rose started working at the hat store and loved it. The previous employee who was having a child, wished to give her baby her fullest attention, and therefore quit earlier than planned. Even better, the store's owner, a wealthy internationalist Italian woman, invited Mary Rose to dinner. Eddie was invited too. Talk had been going on about the dinner for days, as Mary Rose was anxious to make a good impression.

Ramón hadn't been seen in three weeks. Eddie asked no questions about it, preferring to leave him in the past. No other young men had come around, and though Eddie hadn't said anything, he noticed unusually quiet moods from Mary Rose. They bought a goldfish, named him Angel, and Eddie caught her staring into the bowl for long periods of time, obviously not thinking about Angel but something else. Eddie might've attributed these moods to heartsickness, except that between these moments, relaxed smiles were common and eyes softened affectionately when looking his way.

Now wearing the bowtie, feeling even more dapper than before, Eddie stepped from the bedroom a second time and received a delicate smile of approval.

"What hat should I wear?" she asked. "I can't show up without a hat."

She had many hats, all given to her from the store. Clearly, the Italian owner, Abriana, wisely saw Mary Rose as a model, a walking advertisement for the store. Mary Rose explained her dilemma to Eddie. "The pillbox is all the rage in America and Europe, however, in the Latin American market, where the sun is so hot and beating down on you at all times, women prefer a wide brim. Mostly we sell skimmer hats, with the braided straw and flat wide brim. I could wear one of those. Which do you like? A ladies fedora is also popular in the tropics. I could wear that, but I know Abriana would like to sell more of the pillbox hats and the berets. I asked if she ever thought of selling umbrellas in the store, something to go along with the smaller hats, and she said she likes the way I think. I prefer a relaxed looking hat, and feel a wide brim gives a woman a sense of mystery. I'd rather wear one of those but I don't want her to think I'm not interested in selling the others. I think I'll wear one of these skimmers," she decided without input from Eddie.

The restaurant Mary Rose's new boss picked was Con todo mi Corazón on Obispo Street. Abriana and her Cuban husband, Macario, were already finishing a first drink when Eddie and Mary Rose arrived. Abriana smoked with a cigarette holder, had a husky but feminine voice, and clearly was raised in an environment demanding good posture and formal manners. She was beautiful and elegant and gracious, and Eddie liked her immediately. Macario had the aura of an aging Latin film star, impeccably dressed and manicured, he spoke with the richest voice Eddie had ever heard, like he smoked cigars in his sleep. A dark wood setting with exposed wooden ceiling beams boxed warm delicious smells and live Spanish guitar into a cozy haven of revelry and feasting.

Eddie ate a roasted pork sandwich with grilled onions and some kind of terrific tasting sauce. Macario said he liked beer so Eddie had a beer with it. Mary Rose ate grilled white fish. Macario had a pork steak in breadcrumbs but he finished only half of it, and Abriana had roasted chicken with moro rice.

Abriana talked a lot about gloves, how she was bringing a few lines into the store, how clean gloves signified a true lady, and most preferred cream colored or white. Eddie also learned Abriana had a daughter. Was Macario not the father? Eddie didn't want to pry, but it sounded like another man fathered the daughter. The daughter was in boarding school in America, and Macario and Abriana wished to spend more time in America as a result. Therefore, Abriana needed Mary Rose to be mindful of trends so she could possibly assist with buying. She expressed the utmost confidence in her new employee, and Eddie could sense that flattery from such a woman meant a great deal to Mary Rose.

With dishes from the main course removed, they each had some kind of pudding sprinkled with cinnamon, and then the men smoked cigars with strong coffee in little cups. Macario took command of the conversation, asking questions of them, and provided opinions on many topics. Eddie explained to him that he was a dishwasher at the Sevilla-Biltmore, but in a few weeks, he would be transitioning into their accountant.

Though Eddie had shared this news with Mary Rose a week earlier, he never told her how it came about. Apparently, Mr. Castellanos had been sympathetic to the revolution and knew of Alejandro's involvement. Alejandro mentioned to Mr. Castellanos that Eddie—Marty Thorne was the name the Cuban teen used—had a background in banking. What Alejandro secretly referred to when speaking to Mr. Castellanos was the heist, and when he told Eddie this in good humor, he was shocked to learn Eddie actually did have a background in banking for seventeen years. The episode patched up a rough spot between them, though the relationship remained a little tenuous. Even aside from their night at the seawall with Alejandro's mystery friend, complications persisted. Mr. Castellanos once mentioned to Eddie that the mini-operas among kitchen staff erupted due to boredom, and Eddie insinuated to Alejandro that something like that could be a motivating factor behind the more serious turmoil as well. He regretted saying it afterwards as Alejandro became very angry. "Is that what you think? We're bored?" Alejandro had snapped and his eyes narrowed. "He was talking about the dramas in the kitchen," Eddie responded with feigned innocence. "But you brought it up in relation to the revolution."

The simple truth was that Eddie couldn't understand the risks his young friend had been taking, and he wished the violence would end. He sipped his strong coffee and took a puff from an excellent cigar, and drifted back into the conversation by changing the subject to one that had become increasingly important to him. "What do you think of the problems?" he asked Macario. "You know, everything that's been going on."

"I am optimistic," Macario answered thoughtfully. "You have to be. We all have to be, right? Problem is too many lies. One side lies to excuse wealth while doing nothing for the poor. But the other side exaggerates the impoverishment of the Cuban people. We have a city filled with grandeur and wealth. Hundreds of thousands of people live very well here in Havana. We are an energetic, productive, creative people. In the last fifty years, one million Europeans have moved here. Why would they move to a place impoverished? Truth is, you can go block after block after block for miles and see nothing but beautiful architecture. There is a large middle class, one third of the population. In rural areas where so many are cutters, the work is seasonal. They spend a good deal of time out of work. Not their fault. They do nothing wrong but consequently very poor. If subsidized in even a small way the anger would not be so great. As it is, people become convinced they are worse off than they actually are. Compromise is needed. This one gives a little, that one gives a little. Should not be so difficult. The problem is greed, and greed is not a political system. Greed is human nature. Everyone wants more. Some people can never get enough. When those people get in power things become very difficult. That is a time to worry. Although, I do not think things will get more out of hand than already. I suspect there will be compromise and things will calm down eventually. I hope I am right."

Mary Rose had been shy, smiling and nodding modestly throughout the evening's conversation. Now, perhaps more curious about Macario, who Abriana mentioned was an architect when introducing him, she asked, "Did you do many of the buildings around here?"

"Me? No," he answered with some amusement. "They are very old, older than me. Most of my work has been residential properties in Italy."

"Do you like what you do?" Mary Rose asked.

"Architecture is something I am very passionate about. I grew up here in Havana. How could I not dream to be an architect? It is the most beautiful place on Earth. I studied in Germany in the 1920s, but got little from it. I learned mostly by walking the streets of Havana. I am interested in national identity from the perspective of aesthetics. I have always been interested in expanding on tradition without breaking from it. Most architects today, like any artist, wish to tear down tradition, make a clean break from the past. That can work for private art, but architecture of course is a very public art, and a radical departure from the past, too much so, I believe, can be distasteful. You have to look at the whole city, the people and climate. This I learned from the streets of Havana."

"It's interesting," Mary Rose said.

"The other thing that is so important is that artists tend to look beyond their own culture for greatest inspiration. Artists take what inspires them in someone's work from far away. You have to find the balance, as I say, especially in architecture where the works are so public, a balance between new and old, and then seek advancement, not radical departures. Picasso and Matisse did this with painting. They were each inspired by African sculpture, African masks, very much so. They took from Africa in order to give themselves something new, however, what they took was then put into the context of traditional art of western civilization. Wilfredo Lam, the great Cuban painter with ancestral roots in Africa, found inspiration in Picasso without breaking from his own traditions, and consequently the visual language has tremendous authority. They have almost a dialogue, Picasso and Lam, in many of their paintings. It is a truthful conversation because of respect for history and temperament. He is in no way trying to be someone he is not."

Pointedly and politely, Macario then said to Eddie, "I do not mean to talk your ears off if not interesting. Do you know much about what I am saying?"

"No," Eddie admitted. "The only things I know about Africa come from films like *Morocco* and *Algiers*."

"I love those pictures. Of course *Casablanca* was the greatest."

"Perhaps. Although Marlene Dietrich was probably a more interesting female lead in *Morocco* than Ingrid Bergman was in *Casablanca*."

"I agree completely. Dietrich was magnificent in *Morocco*. Every movement, and the clothes, the mystery she conveyed."

"There've been other good ones set in Africa. *The Macomber Affair*."

"As a child, I loved pictures set in cities far away that had a man with some sense of danger about him, some mystery, and he meets a beautiful woman, and there is some adventure, and everything seems to hang by a thread."

"Me too," Eddie said. "*Journey into Fear* was fun. *Singapore* with Fred MacMurray. I like those kinds of movies."

"Love against a backdrop of war, yes." Tapping out his cigar and smiling, Macario said, "If only life could be like the movies."

***

Despite the late hour, Abriana and Macario wished to make an appearance at a party in Vedado. They insisted Mary Rose and Eddie come along, and so they happily did. From Obispo they passed through heavy traffic in Macario's DeSoto Sportsman. Horns blared loudly around them, sounding like trumpets struggling with a new song, and Eddie felt excited to be among such flash and sparkle and neon, so many people in the streets enjoying themselves and acting in defiance of the homemade bombs and Molotov cocktails becoming common. The great congestion of cars was also a beautiful thing to see. Macario said his country imported more American cars than any other country in the world, one hundred and twenty-five thousand Detroit-manufactured vehicles in just over ten years. What did people want with so many cars?

There were buses, and Eddie always liked walking yet they were a joy to see, he thought.

Their friends' home looked like a royal palace. Eddie couldn't believe the magnificence. Waiters balanced trays of champagne among the glittering nouveau riche crowd, while Macario nonchalantly pointed out the tropical and colonial mix of the grand entrance, the stained glass, and he used the word azulejo when referring to walls of glazed ceramic tiles.

A band played. They played the popular music of the island. There was a piano, an upright bass, a trombone and trumpet along with a number of other smaller percussion instruments. Everyone knew Abriana and Macario, and so they were pulled away many times. Some people danced near the band. Perhaps it was the overwhelming sense of everything unfamiliar that made Eddie and Mary Rose suddenly behave like strangers to each other. Awkwardness had slipped between them.

After two more furious numbers, the music slowed considerably. All around Eddie, partners were embraced, couples swayed. Some were elegant and some shuffled clumsily. Eddie felt oafish standing and saying nothing with such a beautiful woman beside him, and so he shrugged and half-smiled, and said, "Would you like to try?"

Eddie's adrenaline jumped as she accepted the invite quickly. For several minutes, they danced without words, focusing instead on their steps, and then Mary Rose brought her soft voice and sweet breath closer to him, and asked, "Why did you agree to come out with me tonight?"

"What do you mean?" Eddie replied. "Why wouldn't I? You invited me."

"Just because I invited you? And so you say yes, just like that?"

"Of course."

A tender smile lifting the corners of her mouth fell and her eyes darkened. "I wish I hadn't hurt you," she said.

"What brings this up?"

"It's just that I, I don't know, I feel like I … messed your life up."

"You didn't mess my life up. Mary Rose, life has been better for me ever since you came along."

"Anybody else would run for the hills."

"That's not true."

"I should've been more honest with you, Eddie. You always deserved that from me. And I blew it a number of times. I don't know what I was thinking. Actually, I do know what I was thinking. I've been thinking back on why I've done some of the things I've done."

"And?"

"Well, I just think that I've … ever since I started working at the store I just feel like I'm at home or something. I feel like I'm doing something that, I don't know, gives me meaning. It makes me feel good about myself. And I guess I've been thinking back on other times and wondering why I made certain choices, and I keep thinking maybe I was running from something, running from certain things in my past. I don't know. Maybe all that running made me feel like that's all I wanted to do, or could do, run. Maybe I don't want to run anymore."

"What are you saying?"

"I'm saying that … Abriana asked about us. She wanted to know if we were getting married someday. I shrugged it off and said we're just friends, and then I started thinking about you and I kept thinking about how, no matter what, you've been there."

"I'm difficult to get rid of."

"I don't believe that. You're a loner. You like to be alone."

"I used to."

For the first time, she tilted her head, leaned in, and kissed him. Her lips triggered a surging from his heart that raced to the most sensitive parts of his face, and when the band shifted their tempo again, it didn't matter.

***

The next morning, as with most mornings, Eddie tried to get some time to think and relax. It had become a necessary part of his day. So much had happened, and he found he needed time to assess what he'd been through. He felt that if he could somehow connect all the past pieces of his life to his present situation, he'd feel more at ease. Yet, no matter how hard he tried, nothing made much sense to him. It was like water running over jagged rocks, he thought; surely he was smoothing them down, but it would take multiple lifetimes for his musings to have any real impact.

He liked to walk. Clarita's Cafe was a favorite spot for breakfast. A sweet old man named Rey served him, and Rey had a handicapped son who lived with him and a face that appreciated even the smallest kindnesses, so Eddie always left a generous tip. On this morning, Eddie had fried eggs, bacon, potatoes and buttered toast with coffee. Some mornings he would have eggs over rice. He did this occasionally when he suspected the bacon and coffee might cause a burning in his stomach. It depended often on what he ate the night before.

Eddie loved the smell of Clarita's. Also, he liked the frenzied activity, the clanging of dishes, the calling out of orders in a foreign language, while he sat calmly detached. It put him in a philosophical mood, helped him relax and think, which is what he'd set out to do.

After breakfast, feeling very satisfied, he walked some more, heading toward the Malecón. He could think and relax even more amidst salty air and a massive amount of sky. Other people walked in twos or threes, he noticed. He overheard three men talking about baseball. Eddie recognized the names of the teams, but not enough of the rest of the words to follow the conversation. Reaching the city's edge, the sky opened completely. He stopped for a moment and put a sheltering hand over his eyes, as the sun was very bright and reflected blindingly off the Caribbean. He then went across to the seawall and sat with his legs hanging freely over the side. The immensity of the sea still captivated him and offered a measure to his insignificance. A small smile formed as he thought back on the kiss Mary Rose had given him.

Eddie then thought back to how he felt the day after Halloween, how nervous he'd been, and how he could only see things then from a very limited view. Heavens to Betsy, was Easter only a week away? Yes, Easter was now only a week away, he reminded himself. He remembered how desperate he'd been to roll the clock back and live the previous night again and again. It was exhilarating to be with Mary Rose then but even better to be with her now.

He couldn't relate to the person he was only five months earlier, and the escapades that carried him from Barstow to Havana hadn't led him to a miserable place. He liked Havana. Strangely, he felt more at ease. He didn't fit in, but unlike where he lived his previous life, he wasn't supposed to fit in. Somehow, that made him more comfortable. What did she feel for him? There seemed to be a growing affection. How long would it last? How long does anything last?

Watching seabirds on secret spy missions for snacks, he thought about the mysterious pull of the ocean. He remembered someone once told him about how waves came from circular motions in the sea. These circular motions moved like giant twirling towers down to the sea floor. As each tower of water approached a landmass, and the depth of the ocean became shallow, the towers would break apart at the bottom, and the top would tumble on to the sand. For a long time, Eddie watched, pondering the repetitiousness of it.

Pivoting finally to the wide road at his back, and all the automobiles speeding past, the great Chariots of Chrome, as someone had called them, Eddie remembered what Macario said about all the cars coming into the country, one hundred and twenty-five thousand in ten years. He suddenly also recollected something Mary Rose once said about Los Angeles.

"Oh, it's really big and wonderful. You've never been?"

"No," Eddie had answered.

"You can't take it all in. You can't see it all. There's so much. There are homes in the mountains and there are stores everywhere. At night, when you're driving down the road it's almost as light as daytime. They sell a lot of cars there. The whole city is packed with cars. There are a lot of sweet little neighborhoods too with little bungalows. It's not hot either, like out here in the desert. It's mild. Sometimes it's even overcast in the morning hours. I like it a lot."

"Did anyone ever ask you to be in the movies?"

"You're so sweet. No. No one ever asked me."

About Stephen Jared

Stephen Jared grew up in a small Ohio town in the late 1970s/early 1980s. He was at the cinema every weekend. When considering what he might do as an adult he only had one idea: he wanted to work in movies. In the summer of 1989 he moved to Los Angeles. He was twenty-one years old. Since then, he's appeared as an actor in movies such as *He's Just Not That Into You,* and on television series such as *iCarly* and *Criminal Minds.*

In 2010, he wrote *Jack and the Jungle Lion,* a novel inspired by 1930s Hollywood. Having received much critical praise, Solstice Publishing began releasing his work, starting with *Ten-A-Week Steale,* hailed as a "fantastic work in the tradition of the old pulp/noir masters." *The Elephants of Shanghai* continued on from where *Jack and the Jungle Lion* left off, and went on to take Second Place at the 2013 Hollywood Book Festival.

While remaining busy as both author and actor, Stephen is also Associate Producer of an upcoming documentary about movie poster artist Richard Amsel who created classic illustrations for *Flash Gordon* and *Raiders of the Lost Ark*, among others, in the late 1970s/early 1980s.

Social Media Links:

Facebook: https://www.facebook.com/stephen.jared.1

Twitter: https://twitter.com/stephen_jared @Stephen_Jared

Website: http://www.stephenjared.com/

Acknowledgements:

Melissa Miller has been more than a publisher. She's been kind, generous and supportive. We all need someone who will give us a chance, and Melissa has always given me a chance. My wonderful wife, Tracy, is enormously helpful and encouraging, and I can't thank her enough for that. Gilles Verschuere, my good friend in Belgium, who published some of my writing years ago, designed the terrific cover for this book. To the readers who've read any of my previous works, I recognize you have a million options, and I appreciate you giving something of mine a shot. – Stephen Jared

If you enjoyed this story, check out these other Solstice Publishing books by Stephen Jared:

The Brutal Illusion

1936. Hollywood. A young woman struggles to fulfill a dream. She meets a man with connections, becomes overjoyed, and soon feels indebted when she lands a studio contract. At the studio, a young writer takes a shine to her; however, rumors circulate that the man who got her the contract is a mobster. Unbeknownst even to her, the rumors are true, and her dream soon becomes a nightmare.

"The heroine's sweet relationship with a screenwriter and the small triumphs and glamour she encounters keep things from becoming unbearably bleak, but it is the dark moments that are the most gripping in this addictive little book." – Classic Film Blog

http://bookgoodies.com/a/B00I805JB4

The Elephants of Shanghai

It's 1942. With war raging, and millions of lives hanging in the balance, the world faces an urgent need for chin-up heroics. Having barely escaped South American headhunters in his last adventure, Jack Hunter seizes the chance to prove his courage. He uses "skills" picked up as a former actor so he can pretend to be a Chicago gangster and pursue spies collaborating with the mob.

A bold plan, however, is not always a clever plan, and when Jack goes missing hope falls on Maxine Daniels, the great love of his life, to pick up a trail that leads all the way to Shanghai, China. Once there, she finds Jack in a race against time involving priceless jewels, secret weapons, a mysterious Chinese singer, and a fiendish warlord.

It's been five years since they survived the Amazon. This time Jack and Max set out to save more than each other – and end up facing a greater danger than they ever could have imagined.

"Jared delivers a fast-paced, old fashioned adventure yarn peppered with just the perfect blend of hair-raising action and laugh aloud comedic bits to help lighten the tension." – Pulp Fiction Reviews

"Jared has a gift for crafting an entertaining plot, with detailed settings that serve to immerse the reader in the time period." – True Classics

http://bookgoodies.com/a/B00COOUJXS

Ten-A-Week Steale

Returned from the Great War, living in 1920s Hollywood, Walter Steale is hired as muscle by his politician brother while a platinum blonde, renowned for playing empty-headed nymphets in the flickers, rekindles his faith in the world. But before long, lies stack up around his work, and Steale finds himself on the front lines of corruption.

Once he confronts his brother, Steale's dirty work is used against him to protect powerful state leaders. Forced into the life of a fugitive, with the secret love of a film star at his side, the former GI fights to expose the state's true enemies while hiding in the shadows of a thriving new metropolis where everyone is dancing fast, chased by sorrow, drugged by the dream of change.

"...a full-throated nostalgia piece. Stephen Jared brings his setting to life with aplomb." – Crime Fiction Lover

"...a fantastic work in the tradition of the old pulp/noir masters." – All Pulp

http://bookgoodies.com/a/B007BQNR6U

www.ingramcontent.com/pod-product-compliance
Lightning Source LLC
Chambersburg PA
CBHW051814020726
47501CB00005B/1509